MW01092150

Acknowledgments

I would like to thank my family for their support through this endeavor. My husband, Keith and my children Kyla and Jaxon's support has been magnificent. You have given me motivation and kept me focused through this time.

I would also like to thank Wanakee for helping me stay on track every step of the way.

My mother Lavoe and my sister's Bianca, Gabrielle, and Viva remind me that my potential can take me far beyond the stars.

Thank you to my little cousin Fior for helping me to recognize my writing potential and my little cousin Blu, for helping to bring that potential to fruition.

Last but certainly not least, I thank my Heavenly Father God, for all my gifts and those who have supported me.

Ratchet/Righteous

Back in the Day

Toni dashed out the screen door and onto the front porch making her grand entrance into the outdoors with her sister and friends. At age ten, she was as tall as an average thirteen year old and as smart as any adult. Needless to say, she was beyond her years in age.

"Get outta my seat." She said in a low threatening tone to her little sister Ivey.

Ivey reluctantly scooted to the left to allow her bossy, manipulative big sister a seat on the top step of the porch. Ivey was only eight but she was smart enough to know that she was not in the mood for a fight, and with Toni she was sure to get one.

"Why you so mean to her?" Red asked with a confused look on her face.

She was tired of Toni mistreating and embarrassing Ivey every chance she got. In her opinion, Ivey was too nice and didn't deserve the treatment that her sister dealt out on a daily basis.

"Cuz."

"Cuz what? Cuz ain't a answer." Red said rolling her neck.

Red was Toni and Ivey's friend that lived down the street. She and her big sister Peaches had been friends with them since they could remember because their parents were acquaintances. But Red was just that, red. She was light skinned like her older sister but there was something in her complexion that turned red when she was upset. She was only eight but she had the temperament of a fire cracker.

"I don't have to answer to you, lil girl!" Toni screamed.

Instantly, Red turned red. She stood up and lifted her hand as far in the air as she could, then sent her skinny fingers crashing into Toni's cheek.

"AAAUGH!" Toni screamed as she held her face in shock.

She couldn't move. She couldn't believe a little girl half her size had the audacity to stand up to her. What she didn't realize is that Red would have stood up to King Kong, she was fearless. Even Red's parents had a hard time containing the time bomb. At that moment Red began to growl like a rabid dog and charged Toni knocking them both off the porch and into the grass. Toni was caught off guard, but she was hardly afraid. The neighborhood kids watched as Peaches and Ivey struggled to break up the brawl, but were unsuccessful. They fought like two grown men until they finally grew tired. Ivey tried to catch her breath and stood off to the side with a slight smirk on her face because Red had actually gotten the best of Toni, and she felt it was greatly deserved and definitely appreciated.

Lois, Toni and Ivey's mother, stepped outside just as the fight was dying down.

"What the hell is going on out here?" She screamed.

"Red and Toni fighting!" The children outside sang in unison.

"Get your behind in the house!" Lois yelled while motioning Toni inside.

"And you!" She pointed to Red, "Go home, now! I'm calling your mother."

Lois didn't care why they were fighting. All she knew is she did not approve of friends getting physical and she hated for young women to fight one another. She always said you should preserve your beauty as long as you can.

Lois was beautiful. She stood six feet tall and could put Beverly Johnson to shame. She was the true definition of a stallion. Her caramel complexion was flawless and accompanied by her deep set slanted eyes, gave her an exotic look that could easily have been mistaken for someone from the islands.

She sat silently at first, wiping blood and dirt out of Toni's scratches. She had already spoken to Red's mother Brenda and found out the fight started because of Red trying to defend Ivey. So Toni is faced with the question again.

"So, why are you so mean to her?" Lois asked.

"Huh?" Toni looks up to face her mother.

"Your sister, why are you so mean to her?"

"I just be playing with her, momma." Toni said with the innocence of an angel.

"It's not playing if you're the only one getting enjoyment out of it. And furthermore, that is your only sister, your blood. One day she might be all you have. You have to stop mistreating her."

Up until this point in their lives, Toni had been as abusive as one child could be to another. She use to pinch and hit Ivey as a baby, and now that they were older Toni took every opportunity she could to try to pick fights or degrade Ivey in the presence of other children.

Lois knew there was a problem but was unaware of how much of a problem it was because Ivey never told. In fact, Ivey would do anything for Toni, regardless to what she did. Lois just feared that one day Toni's luck would run out and her little sister will not be as easily bullied and manipulated as she is as a child. Lois kept them in church and let them know the importance of having a spiritual foundation. She also wanted her girls to know the importance of family and loyalty to friends, but she was slowly coming to realize that Toni would live by rules of her own.

Thirteen years later

Red: Doesn't always mean stop

Red stood in the middle of the floor of the honeymoon suite at the Four Seasons in New York City. She walked to the full length mirror admiring the sexy attire that Mr. Grant had delivered to her suite. Mr. Grant was the CEO of Affinity Entertainment, which was one of the largest entertainment corporations on the east coast. Red hooked up with him at an industry party she crashed at the Plaza Hotel in New York. She made a name for herself by associating with the "right" people and being at right place at the right time. She had a knack for that. Plus, her Bachelor's degree in Communications made her as versatile as a chameleon. No one could tell her family was as ghetto as "The Jerry Springer Show".

She wasn't the type to sleep with a bunch of rappers and grimy niggas, so she called them. She would strategically place herself around what she called the "white money". While the rappers and R&B types associated with one another, she made sure to catch the attention of the men that signed their paychecks.

"Hello beautiful." Mr. Grant says, noticing her double D sized implants.

"Hello yourself." Red responded with a sexy shrug of her shoulder.

She wasn't exactly a dime and she knew it, but she also knew how to entice the type of men she wanted to put her hooks into. She was slender with not much curves except the ones on her chest. And although she was only five foot seven, the six inch Manolo Blahniks she sported made her look like a stallion. Her bright yellow complexion would sometimes allow her to be mistaken for white, from across the room. The blonde, waist length sew in that she kept super tight didn't help in the misconception either.

"Are you here alone?" Mr. Grant asks her.

"Not if I'm here with you." She smiled.

Her dark cat shaped eyes made her mysterious, but the see through Gucci dress left nothing to the imagination.

"Well then, you're in good company. Can I buy you a drink?"

"Yes, Cabernet Sauvignon, please." She sang.

The gentleman left and returned with their drinks.

"So, who may I have the honor of saying is accompanying me tonight?" he asked.

"Drea Mason, but my friends call me Red." She extended her hand.

"Well, my name is Jonathan Grant, but my friends call me John." He was still holding her hand in his.

She wasn't the most beautiful woman in the world but he was awestruck by her presence alone.

"I would prefer Mr. Grant, if you don't mind?" she asked.

"Why so formal? I was hoping that we would become friends."

"It's not about formalities, it's about power. Mr. Grant exudes power. And I want you to feel as powerful as possible in my presence." She whispered in his ear as she leaned closer with every word.

His medium sized erection instantly became apparent and he shifted in his seat before it was noticed. But what he didn't know was that Red knew exactly what she was doing. She knew his penis was erect just like she knew she could have him wrapped around her finger, as she notices the tan line around the finger where his wedding ring should have been.

*"Yes, just like I like em', white, married, old, and rich!"
she thought to herself as she made Mr. Grant
comfortable about what was going on in his pants.*

*"Don't worry Mr. Grant, you're with me tonight." She
gave him a wink.
That was two years ago, and their affair has been going
on ever since.*

Knock! Knock! Knock! She was jarred from her
memory.
She took one last look in the mirror, and then headed to
the door.

"Entrée", she said in her best French accent while she
ushered Mr. Grant into her suite.

"Merci", He replied with an instant look of lust in his
eyes at the sight of Red in the see through robe and
thong, not to mention the come fuck me red bottom
pumps he had delivered to her suite earlier that day.

He was always excited to see Red. She was always
attentive to ALL of his needs. Unlike his grumpy
alcoholic wife who had grown tired of pleasing him in
any way a long time ago. So Red gladly stepped in
where she left off, bank account and all.

Mr. Grant was not an attractive man, but he made up for
it in class. He was a stocky built gentleman of about five
foot seven inches tall, with mingly gray hair. He was
always well dressed and smelled good, but he was as

hairy as King Kong. Although she didn't complain because he kept her draped and her bank account fat. Not only was she paid for the "special favors" she did for him, but also the gigs he got her hooked up with. Music videos were her main source of income. He would connect her with the most lucrative videos and the most famous clients. His only rule was that she not sleep with any of his artist. Outside of that, she could deal with whomever she pleased. And up to this point, there has been no one more important than her money.

"Have a seat sweetheart." She said while grabbing his tie and leading him to the beautiful antique sofa.

His favorite cognac, 1738 Remy Martin, was already chilling at the bar. Red handed him a drink on the rocks, just the way he liked it. She then proceeded to remove his shoes and socks to massage his short fat feet. He was in heaven. No one made him feel like she did. She would do what he wanted without having to ask. It was like she was reading his mind. But to her, he wasn't that hard to read. He just wanted what all men wanted, to feel like a king.

"How was your flight baby?" Red asked.

"It was okay, I couldn't wait to see you though." He smiled.

"Well your wait is over. Any requests?" She pointed to the radio.

"Something smooth and sexy." He said.

Red had to contain her laughter as she walked to the radio to put on some jazz, because he was the unsexiest thing she had ever seen. Sade Smooth Operator softly played in the background as Red turned and slowly began to strip out of her robe. Mr. Grant's nature rose as her breast popped from inside of the sheer garment. By this time, he was kicking off the perfectly pressed slacks he wore into a ball on the floor. Needless to say, he was excited.

"You ready to taste this pussy, Mr. Grant?" She asks.

He loved when she called him that since the first time they met.

"Please." He begged.

All he knew was, she had the sweetest pussy he ever tasted, literally. Unbeknownst to him she had been putting apple Jolly Ranchers inside her ever since she found out the effect it had on men.

In her next motion, she took off her shoes and stood over Mr. Grant on the sofa. Instinctively, he tilted his head back in anticipation of what was next. Red bent her knees slowly, dangling her wetness above his lips and tongue. She was teasing him and he loved it. Although he wasn't sexy, her juices increased at the thought of his head game, it was fire. She figured he was making up for the size of his dick. Finally, she rested her knees on the back of the sofa and allowed his lips to kiss hers. He sucked her clit into his mouth and tongue kissed it with care. Her sexy moans cause him to stroke his dick. He took his free hand and stuck two fingers into her wetness. She was a squirter and he loved it. Her body began to shutter as her climax came to a head. She released a flood of juices into his mouth and onto his face and he lapped up every drop he could catch.

Red reached between the sofa cushions to retrieve the condom she had placed there earlier. She got down on her knees to remove his boxers to reveal his medium sized monster. His penis was uncircumcised and as ugly as they come, so a condom was a must, even when she gave him head. It didn't make a difference to him though because her head game was off the charts, she was a master.

She placed the condom around her lips and on her tongue then put her lips on the head of his dick. She rolled the condom down his shaft with her lips and tongue. He was already losing it. By the time she made it to the base, she was slightly humming and running her tongue up and down the length of his dick while cupping his balls. He was in heaven. Red could tell by the force in his thrust and the tightness of his nuts that he was close to cuming.

Then seemingly in one motion, she stood up and straddled his manhood. Her tight twenty one year old pussy was as juicy as a peach and just as good. She rode him like he had the best dick ever while he took both her breast in his hands and took turns sucking each one hungrily. He had to stop from screaming out as his nut filled the condom. They sat there in the same position for a few moments sweating and panting.

Finally Red went to the bathroom to retrieve a wet towel. She cleaned Mr. Grant's penis from the scrotum to the tip.

"You're so good to me." Mr. Grant said while admiring Red's naked body.

"You deserve everything I give you daddy." Red said kissing his nose after finishing his wash up. "I'm not done with you yet."

She was sure he had taken a double dose of Viagra before coming to see her and she sexed him until the wee hours of the morning. By the next morning she was $20,000 richer with a job that paid that much more. They ended their visit with breakfast in bed and a transfer of funds to her bank account. Oh how she loved Mr. Grant!

Toni Toni Toni!

"Bitch suck this dick!" Romero said with a hand full of Toni's long thick hair. She loved it when he talked to her that way when they made love, if that's what you want to call it. And he loved the fact that she was freaky enough to like it.

Toni was pretty much devoted to one person…..herself. But if she had to say she was loyal to anyone it would be Romero Wallace or Rome as she called him. He was the closest thing she had to a man, but even he couldn't tame her. She lost respect for pretty much everything and everyone after her mother Lois died when she was eighteen. She had always blamed her father for her mother and his divorce, and even more for her suffering when she died of complications from Lupus. His way of handling despair was absence, so they never developed much of a relationship after he left their home. So up until this point in her life, she has had a fuck the world mentality.

"Aaaaahhhh!" Rome growled as he released his seed into Toni's mouth. She swallowed every drop. "You nasty bitch." He said with an almost endearing tone. "You tryna make a nigga fall in love?"

"Wha….aw fuck naw! And you betta not say no shit like that no more! You know I ain't tryna give a fuck about shit out here. But that is my dick though." She smiled playfully, but still very serious about her previous comment and he knew it.

"When yo ass gone settle down and let a nigga take care of all dat?" Rome said pointing at her six foot one inch frame from head to toe.

Rome knew Toni was a free spirit and he accepted her for whom and what she was. He was actually in love with her. But, because of her demeanor he would never tell her, because she would perceive him as weak.

"You already taking care of all of this." She said pointing to herself from head to toe with sass that only she could personify.

Toni was referring to the money and sex he provided but Rome was referring to something altogether different and certainly more serious. While Rome had a soft spot for Toni, he was still a man that would confront and even kill anyone that crossed him the wrong way. He ran the streets and his business did not allow for any cowardice.

One of the things he admired about Toni was the fact that she had heart and street smarts, on top of being scholastically intelligent. She was substantially younger he was, she was only twenty three and he was well into his thirties. Initially he thought that Toni would be easy to control because of her age, but he was sadly mistaken. She was nineteen when they met and one of the feistiest women he had ever known. He was instantly smitten with the youngster that had the soul of a gangster.

Although Rome was twelve years her senior, at thirty five he was still at the prime of his life. Rome was about six foot five and could have easily been mistaken for an NBA player with his basketball player physique. He had a Hershey caramel complexion with the chiseled features of a GQ model. But his eyes were as dark and mysterious as his voice. Actually, depending on who you were and what he was discussing with you, it could be the sexiest or the most terrifying experience of your life. He was definitely a force to be reckoned with. This is what had initially drawn Toni to him; the fact that he was hood rich was a plus.

"What time does my flight leave?" Toni asked referring to her flight back to St. Louis from Atlanta.

Rome had moved there after evading the Feds in St. Louis, with the luck of the Irish. One of the street boys got caught by the police and Rome was sure he would snitch. What Rome didn't know was how far his power in the streets ran. Even snitches were afraid to snitch on him, so the Feds were never able to get any witnesses to his actions. Romero was too smart for them to obtain evidence, so witnesses were all they had, so they thought.

Despite the police not having a case, Rome decided it would be best to relocate. There was no need to start over because he still maintained the same connects and the same clients.

Romero admired Toni's long curvy frame as she sashayed around the room gathering her belongings.

"I'm having Jojo drop you off at the airport at 7pm, your flight leaves at 8:30pm. We still got time for one more round." Rome looked down at the tent forming in his jogging pants.

Toni got wet at the thought of fucking and sucking him, he knew how to please her. He was the perfect combination of rough and sensual. He would handle her gently right before he smacked her ass and pulled her hair. She smiled at the thought. Then she dropped her pile of clothes and straddled him all in the same motion.

"You better hope I don't miss my flight." She said into his mouth before tonguing him down and releasing the beast from his jogging pants.

"Did you get the information I asked you for?" Toni asked Jojo nonchalantly while digging around in her Louis Vutton travel case.

Jojo was Peaches alleged babies' daddy. Peaches wasn't as thorough as her little sister Red when it came to men.

She dealt with bottom of the barrel thugs and Jojo was the best of a bad situation. Jojo was Rome's right hand man and partner, but his money wasn't as long as Rome's. Romero actually knew how to handle his money and was looking into opening a night club in Atlanta, whereas, Jojo was looking for the newest pair of Jordans.

"Yeah, Peaches said her and Red got a job on a video set for Ludacris. She said its set for next week in Cali." He snitched.

"Good, I need all the info. I need the location, the time, and what kind of attire. I'm a have to crash the set. Them bitches won't help me get on, so I'm a have to help myself." She said matter of factly.

"Whatchu gone give me?" Jojo looked at Toni with lust in his eyes.

"You bitch ass nigga! What the fuck you think this is? I been with Rome all week, you know I'm not about to fuck you! Its rules to this shit!" Toni screamed.

As tough as Jojo was, Toni always created a slight nervousness in his gut when she got upset. Something about her told him that her 'I don't give a fuck' attitude, was not an act. He had been sleeping with Toni for about six months now, and he loved it. She was a certified freak and he understood Romero's obsession with her. Neither of them cared what Peaches thought if she found out, but Rome was another story. They both knew they would die before he tolerated that kind of disloyalty in his circle. That was the number one reason Toni made rules. There was to be no contact immediately before or after she was with Rome. She didn't want him to smell Jojo on her or vice versa. That's why Jojo's advance toward her was not only unwanted but also unwelcomed. "How dare he!" was all she could think, ignoring the fact that she was as wrong in this situation as he was.

"My bad, damn! And watch yo mutha fuckin tone in my ride!" He tried to get aggressive.

"Yeah whateva nigga, you just make sure you get me that info. You get this," She said pointing to her crotch. "When I get that." Were her last words as she exited Jojo's Camaro and walked toward the airport entrance.

"Crazy bitch!" Jojo shook his head as he pulled off.

Jo and Rome

Growing up in the Peabody Projects of St. Louis was no cake walk. It was especially difficult if your support system was zero. Jojo moved in with Romero and his mother Lisa when he was fourteen years old. His mother Trisha had been strung out on drugs ever since he could remember so when she stopped coming home and the bills stopped being paid, he was forced out into the streets.

He and Romero had been friends since first grade and were brothers as far as they were concerned. Romero's brother Rio had been killed in a drug deal gone badly two years prior and Jojo had no siblings that he knew of, so Lisa was more than happy to take in the boy she already considered a son.

"Man I'm finna get this money, I'm sick of dis shit." Said a fourteen year old Romero looking at his beat up tennis shoes.

"Moms ain't finna stand for dat shit and you know it." Jo said looking down at his own raggedy set of shoes.

"Why you acting like a pussy. We can make enough money to get all our ass up outta here." Rome said referring to the projects in general.

"Bro, I'm down witchu whateva, but I love yo mom like she mine and after what happened to Rio."

"I ain't no mutha fuckin Rio." Rome angrily cut him off in mid-sentence. "He wasn't smart about his shit. And with all that money he made, he didn't do shit for us, just like that nigga!" Rome screamed referring to his absentee father Rio Sr. "I'll never abandon my seed, that's some punk shit." Romero had calmed down, but still spoke with as much emotion as he stared down at his bedroom floor.

"Me either dog." Jojo understood more than he wanted to.

Jojo had no idea who his father was and was much less aware of where to find his mother.

"But for real though, dis nigga Pookie said he would front me if I wanna get on. So wuz good, you got my back?" Rome stared into Jojo's eyes and waited for his response.

Jojo and Romero, although two of the youngest, were also among the most feared in their neighborhood, so his hesitation had to do with only one thing, his mother. He never wanted to contribute to the misfortune he was dealt. And although he was grateful for his surrogate family, he had to adapt to his situation.

"I'm down, it's me and you man." Jo finally said to Rome as they gave one another a brotherly pound.

They were inseparable then and even though their empire had relocated, they've been that way ever since.

Five years later, Jojo got the news that his mother had been found strangled to death in North St. Louis. And later that year, Lisa died of a heart attack. They were brothers bonded by friendship, and tragedy made them closer that partners, they were family.

My sister's keeper

Ivey pulled up to the East Terminal of the St. Louis Lambert Airport to pick up her sister, Toni. She watched as Toni exited the airport doors. She always admired her sister's beauty. To her, Toni resembled a runway model and looked the most like their mother, in her opinion. She had a milk chocolate complexion with exotic facial features like their mother, with thick hair that hung to the middle of her back. She always appeared confident and carefree, but Ivey knew there was so much more behind who Toni actually was. They were close and distant at the same time. Toni would tell Ivey about some of the things going on in her life, but cared enough about her sister not to expose her to it. Or, she just didn't want the competition. Which one, was yet to be determined in Toni's mind.

"What up chick?" Toni said as she hopped into the passenger's seat of Ivey's new mustang.

"Cayute!" She said as she admired the interior of Ivey's ride.

"Nothing and thank you!" Ivey squealed. "So how's Rome and Jojo and Atlanta?" Ivey asked.

Toni thumbed through her text messages. She had just received the information she requested from Jojo about the video shoot. She pressed "save" as she answered casually.

"Aw, they cool. Ain't nothing new. What's up with school?" Ivey was getting her bachelor's degree in psychology at Saint Louis University.

"I just finished my final and I'm so ready to graduate. I wish mom could be here." Ivey's mood changed.

"Girl! Quit crying over spilled milk and shit! You blowin' highs. Besides, I'll be there. You talk to daddy?" Toni asked as if it hurt her throat to ask about him.

"Naw, I left a couple of messages for him though. I'm sure he's afraid to be in the same vicinity as you since that fiasco as my high school graduation." Ivey reminded Toni.

After their mother died, their father Randy left them with their maternal grandmother. And although they loved their Mee Maw Gloria, Toni always felt Randy was more than selfish for leaving them without a mother or father, or without a choice for that matter. So when Toni was in her father's presence, it was impossible to contain her anger, so she didn't. And until their grandmother died a year before, Mee Maw Gloria had the only respect Toni had to give.

Randy Danes was the sole reason Toni had so little respect for men. She felt if her own father would abandon her, then another man could care less. Therefore, emotions were not an option. In fact, there were times when Toni didn't care much about anything, including life. Unbeknownst to anyone in her life, Toni had attempted suicide on several occasions. But when she kept waking up alive, she stopped trying. Now she just lived like she's ready to die.

Now Ivey on the other hand, was a ray of sunshine. She had dealt first hand with everything that Toni endured, however, her outlook on life was the complete opposite. Ivey saw the bright side of things and could make the best of a bad situation. Considering growing up with Toni was not easy, she had to learn to adjust to controversy and create a happy existence inside of living with the nightmare that was Toni. But despite all that, Ivey loved her sister immensely.

"Well, if he shows up, he'd better not bring that bitch." Toni said referring to Regina, Randy's wife.

 Toni refused to acknowledge her as a step mother or anything for that matter. She simply couldn't understand how a woman would allow a man to abandon his children. The thought of them both disgusted her.

"I'm sure no one wants a twelve round title match at the graduation, so I'm sure she won't show and I'm still

questionable about dad. Anyway, wanna do lunch?"
Ivey asked her sister.

"That's cool, just run me by my apartment so I can drop
off this bag and freshen up." Toni said.

Toni lived in the Metroloft building in the Central West
End, which was right down the street from their favorite
sushi restaurant, Subzero. So it was perfect. They had
lunch and talked like normal siblings. These were the
times Ivey cherished with her sister. No hate, no
animosity, and no arguing. Ivey cherished every
moment, because she knew any stability on Toni's behalf
was definitely short lived. So Ivey did her best to make
time stand still.

Not So Georgia Peach

"Get yall shit together and quit playing!" Peaches screamed at her children Raina and Ryan from her bedroom.

Ryan was four and Raina was three. Peaches was the kind of mother that made a child want to raise themselves. She was not at all nurturing and even less maternal.

"Where is this nigga?" She said out loud in frustration. She was anticipating Jojo's arrival for more reasons than one.

First and most importantly, he was coming to get the children she couldn't stand to be around. Partially because she knew the man taking care of her children was not their father. It was almost like she blamed them for not looking like him. Not to mention the fact that she was not at all cut out be a mother.

And as if they were the ones that lay down and got pregnant twice, she also blamed them because she didn't do more with her life. Although she was only five foot five inches tall and short for a model, she had been told on numerous occasions that she was pretty enough to become one. She was actually very gorgeous.

She was light complected with a kiss of honey. Her almond brown hair with natural blonde streaks lay in layers down her back. She knew it was a big deal to men that her hair wasn't weave, so she made it a point to wear it down as often as possible. She had round hazel green eyes and full lips. One would think she was of Latin decent. Her body was as curvaceous as an hour glass, which made her the envy of women and got the full attention of any man. Her real name was Deanna, but Peaches was a nickname given to her as a child because of her skin color, but other than the name, there was nothing soft about her.

"Daddy!" Peaches heard the children scream from the other room. She had given Jojo a key to the section 8 apartment in O'fallon Place ever since he started paying her rent. So, if she had the urge to test the waters elsewhere, he'd better be prepared to spring for a room. Peaches refuse to jeopardize her cash cow for anybody. Just as he hit the corner of her bedroom door, she remembered the other reason she was eagerly awaiting his arrival.

He was one of the finest, black chocolate men she had ever seen, not to mention, extra sexy. Jojo was six foot one with the natural physique of a god. His chocolate skin was flawless, all except the gun hot wound on the inside of his thigh. He was hung like a horse, so anyone in a position to see his wound, their attention would quickly be diverted. Her clit throbbed at the thought of it.

"Whatchu in here doin mah?" Jojo asked Peaches.

"Um, packing? What it look like?" She said holding up her partially filled garment bag. She turned and faced the bed with her back to Jojo and continued packing.

Jo stood in the doorway admiring her plump, round, apple shaped ass in her black, Love Pink boy shorts. He thought Peaches was one of the finest women he knew. But he also realized that beauty was only skin deep. Jo wasn't at all stupid, so he knew Peaches was not girlfriend material. He even knew that the chances of her children being his were slim to none but he was there for both their births and cut the cords, so he had a paternal attachment to them. They were both very light skinned with blue gray eyes and actually the cutest kids he had ever seen. He was proud to say they were his and had actually grown to love Raina and Ryan. He gave them those names.

"See something you like?" Peaches asked, shaking her butt in his direction, jarring him from his thoughts.

"Hell yeah! I like all of it. Who you been giving my pussy to?" He walked closer to her as he spoke. She turned to look into his deep dark eyes. His eyelashes

31

were long and thick, which made his stare as effective as his tongue.

"Nobody." She lied in a whisper with her head tilted back as he stroked her already protruding clit through her shorts. She was starting to soak through her garment when she heard her bedroom door close and lock. "What about the kids?" She panted almost ready to cum from his touch.

"I just wanna taste it." He said in a low, sexy baritone voice.

He was actually trying to save himself for Toni. Peaches and Toni were both freaks, but Toni picked up and ran, where Peaches left off. But Jo loves sucking Peaches' peach. Her reaction made him feel like the king of the world. Peaches lay on her back as Jo crawled between her thighs. He put his arms beneath her legs and held her wrists so she couldn't run. Her parted her lips with his tongue and slowly teased her clit. Her pussy pulsated with every stroke and she could hardly contain the sounds coming from her throat. She tried to be quiet, but his mouth was so good, she was on the verge of screaming.

Just as he thought, she started trying to push his head away, but his grip wouldn't allow it. She fought to get her hands free and pumped his face at the same time. Her body began to shake and he released her hands as she released. Before she could recover, Jo was already in the children's room helping them finish packing. He was taking them back to Atlanta while Peaches went to the video shoot in California with Red.

The average mother would have been worried or at least attempted to say goodbye. But the reality was, he was a far better father than she was a mother, and they both knew it.

After basking in the glow of "good head", Peaches heard the front door close and lock. She went to the living room, then the children's room. Empty. She returned to the living room and noticed ten crisp one hundred dollar bills on the coffee table. Next to the money was a note that read:

Thanks for the Peach :) Be safe.
See you in two weeks
Jojo

First day of forever

Brandon had butterflies in his stomach as he pulled in front of Ivey's condo in North County. He had been dating her for the past two years and knew he would never love another woman this much. She was his soul mate. He knew it sounded cliché, but they, were no cliché. Their love was as real as God in his opinion.

To him Ivey was beautiful inside and out. She had smooth caramel skin that looked like a constant sun tan. She had honey blonde locks that reached the middle of her back. Her five foot ten inch frame was slender but she lacked nothing in the chest area and her long legs seemed to start at her neck. Ivey had a small butt and hips that were just right to Brandon. He preferred a smaller more petite frame, and hers was perfect for him. He loved her slanted almond colored eyes. They were his favorite part of her, besides her heart. Her eyes seemed to smile at him at every glance and the dimples that appeared when she smiled with her full lips, just added to the butterflies he got every time he saw her.

They met at the school library reaching for the same book and they've been a match made in heaven ever since. He graduated the year before and was eagerly awaiting Ivey's graduation. He was proud of her and looked up to her for accomplishing so much without her parents in her life. He came from a very close knit family with both parents. Brandon was the youngest of three boys, and he could totally relate to being picked on by older siblings. That also gave him a soft spot when it came to Ivey.

He nervously rang the doorbell and waited for Ivey to answer. She opened the door with gracefulness and the beauty of an angel. She wore all white, a sheer white BeBe blouse with a white cami underneath. She also wore white slacks and white Gucci wedges. She didn't care much for labels, but as her mother had always told them, "Always keep a few items of good quality." She taught them that they could mix and match them with less expensive items and people would be none the wiser.

Her hair was pulled back into a bun giving her a sophisticated look. Brandon told her they had reservations at a five star restaurant, so she wanted to dress the part.

"Hey babe." Ivey said as she planted a kiss on Brandon's lips.

"Hey beautiful!" Brandon responded.

Ivey admired Brandon wearing his seersucker ensemble. He was a handsome specimen of a man. He was six foot two with and athletic physique. He kept a Caesar haircut and a goat tee that rivaled Idris Elba's. He was brown with deep, dark, sexy eyes and a slight dimple in his chin.

"You ready to go?" Brandon asked.

"Yep." Ivey said then grabbed her blazer and headed out the door.

The car ride was awkward and silent. They held hands like they always did, but Brandon was unusually quiet.

"Baby, you okay?" Ivey asked.

"I'm perfect." He said

"Well you're awfully quiet." She said squeezing his hand.

"Just thinking. Everything's fine. I have you, it's a beautiful day, and we're blessed. I don't have any complaints." Brandon smiled at Ivey while gently squeezing her hand back.

"Okay then Mr. Serenity, where are you taking me?"

"J. Gilberts." He said pointing to the sign of the restaurant while he pulled up to the valet.

"Oh, how bushee!" She laughed.

As they entered, Brandon gave his name to the matre'd.

"Reservations for B. Cameron? Right this way." The small blonde man led them to an elevated booth next to a large fire place.

"This is beautiful." Ivey said in awe. She then thumbed through the menu and noticed the entrees cost more than any meal she had ever eaten or paid for, for that matter.

"Um, have you looked at this menu?" She said still looking at the prices in amazement.

Brandon however, could not take his eyes off of Ivey. Finally he spoke as if almost in a trance.

"Don't worry about that, you're worth every penny. Order what you want." He told her.

They ordered fillet mignon and lobster with a glass of Cabernet Sauvignon to complement their meal. After they laughed, talked and enjoyed each other's company, Ivey ate her last bite of steak.

"It's like butter baby." Ivey sighed, rubbing her stomach.

Brandon couldn't contain his laughter as he watched Ivey's slim waist stretch to look like she was carrying a small fetus.

"Did you enjoy?" He laughed.

"That is a severe understatement Mr. Cameron. What did I do to deserve this anyway?" Ivey asked with suspicion.

Just then, Brandon stood up with a small black box and got down on one knee. Ivey clasped her hands over her mouth. She was in shock. She pinched her own arm to make sure she wasn't dreaming. "Ouch!"

"The day I met you, I realized what I'm supposed to do with my life, and that's not to live one more day without you in it. I love you more than I ever knew possible to love another person. God said "He who finds a wife, finds a good thing." But when I found you I found something beautiful. Will you, Ivey Danes, please do me the honor of being my wife?"

"A million times YES!"

Girls Night Out

Toni had spoken to Peaches several times since finding out about the video shoot, but Peaches had still failed to mention anything about it. Toni figured she would give Peaches one last chance to invite her to the shoot before she took it upon herself to crash it.

They were all getting money together at one point, so it was baffling to Toni why she suddenly stopped being invited to go do the shoots. She figured jealousy had to be the culprit. The fact that she went into the shoots as if she was Queen Bee and the director wrapped all in one, never crossed her mind. She knew she was a diva, but she figured everyone else knew it too, and accepted it as fact.

Toni and Peaches made plans to go out to the Coliseum Night Club. It was a pretty big place and Toni loved the attention she got when she entered a crowded room. For at least the first ten seconds, it's like she's the only woman present. It was a small shot of adrenaline.

They decided to meet at Toni's place since she didn't live very far from the club. Toni's phone rang and she buzzed Peaches into the building. Moments later, Toni heard a light knock.

"It's open!" She yelled, still in the bathroom perfecting her makeup.
"Hey lady!" Toni said with a fake smile. "Fire up that blunt in there in the ashtray." She pointed to the living room. She admired Peaches' attire as she turned to go retrieve the ashtray.

Peaches wore an off white DKNY jumper. The drawstring made her small waist appear smaller and her large butt seem even larger. Toni was confident about every aspect of herself, so even Peaches' shapely showoff outfit couldn't make her fell like the less attractive of the two. Toni sported a white sleeveless Narisco Rodriguez dress. It was a transparent sheath dress that hugged every curve of her body. So she didn't feel shabby in the least.

"What's up with Ivey? I haven't talked to her in about a month." Peaches inquired.

"Girl you know she booed up. Between school, church, and that nigga, I hardly see her myself. Speaking of little sisters, what's up with Red? I haven't heard from her since we did the video in Atlanta. That was like two months ago. She cool?" Toni asked, trying to lead Peaches.

"Yeah, she straight. You know she don't ever sit still. I'm going to see her in New York this weekend. I just need to get away from them kids." Peaches lied.

"Damn! What happened to the work? You bitches retired or something?" Toni said looking at Peaches over her shoulder as she passed her the blunt and waited for an answer.

"Look, I got kids and I don't know what Red is doing!" Peaches said defensively.

"Slow down slut! I just asked a question. No need for all the defense. Well, since you're going to see her, let her know I asked about her." Toni decided she didn't want Peaches' guard up at all. She wanted to strike with the precision of a viper. Quickly, quietly, and completely by surprise.

Toni and Peaches arrived at the club just before they would be forced to stand outside in a long line. Just as always when the two women walked inside the club, it was like a real life sized chocolate banana sundae had grown legs and walked in the building. Men and women's jaws dropped. Only the women too insecure to give them their props, sucked their teeth in disgust. Women hated them and they loved it.

They made their way to the booth that Toni reserved for them in advance. The waiter approached the table with a bottle of Remy Martin, two glasses, and a bucket of ice. The two rocked to the music and sipped their drinks while men of every caliber did everything to gain either of the women's attention, without looking like chumps. They had taken away the men's power to approach them. They had their own seat, their own money, and their own drinks. So the only thing left to do was to approach them like real men or keep it moving.

"Well, well, well, look at this bitch chillin' in the club like shit's sweet." Toni turned her head toward a familiar female voice.

It was Coco. She met her out at a strip club and thought she was cool to hang with until she began to become possessive. Plus, she had too many kids and too many babies' daddies. She had too much going on and not enough help as far as Toni was concerned.

"Don't come over here with that shit." Toni observed Coco looking like she had received a hood rat makeover.

She was dark skinned, about five foot seven and thin as spaghetti. So everything she had on was too tight and too small.

"And who is this, yo bitch? You know I know how you get down." Coco questioned Toni about Peaches.

"Hold up! You doing way too much! Don't get yo ass whooped on no bullshit! Speak yo peace. What do you want?" Toni screamed.

Peaches looked at them both in confusion. Then finally after an uncomfortable few seconds, Coco finally said.

"You'll find out soon enough, you dike bitch." Then Coco turned and slowly walked away.

"What the fuck?" Peaches questioned.

"Fuck that crazy bitch." Toni told Peaches, raging mad on the inside. Toni was ready to pounce. But she wasn't sure what Coco's issue was, so she thought it best to wait.

"Another time, another place." Toni said to herself. "Another time."

Cali Love

It was 3:30 am and her flight left at 5 am. Toni loaded her car and headed to short parking at the airport. All she could think about was crushing Peaches and Red's dreams when she arrived at Luda's video shoot. She made sure to shop for the sexiest gear, get a fresh razor haircut, manicure and pedicure, and she got her eyebrows threaded. She was flawless.

As she pulled onto I-170 north, she noticed she had been followed since she got on Forest Park Expressway. Continuing on her journey, she was sure to take note of the blue Mercedes truck with the license plate ending in 678 as she drove. Just as she pulled into the short term parking entrance, the truck kept straight. She gave a sigh of relief as she found a parking space and waited for the shuttle to her airline.

LA

Toni exited the terminal at LAX and looked for the space that held her rental car. The sun shined brighter than she could ever remember seeing the sun shine. She loved LA and couldn't wait to paint the town red.

She pulled out her phone and noticed several missed calls from Ivey.

"I'll call her after the shoot." She said as she went to retrieve the addresses to her intended locations from her phone; first her hotel, The Hollywood, then the video location.

Since dealing with Rome, Toni had established connections in just about every major city in the country. But when she traveled with him, it was always business and never pleasure. This time she would be mixing a little bit of both. So she hooked up with Smokey, for just that, smoke.

She got her cush fix and was ready to get dolled up for her grand entrance. Back at her suite, she laid out several outfits and jumped in the shower. As she washed away her airplane ride, Toni thought back to the blue Mercedes truck. She could remember seeing the truck somewhere before, but was having the hardest time remembering where. It had to have been a while, so whoever it was, was in serious need of an upgrade in her opinion.

As she finished showering, she heard Sister Sledge "We Are Family" playing, so she knew Ivey was calling again. She jumped out of the shower and ran to the bedside table to retrieve her IPhone.

"Hey Chic." Toni sang as she answered.

"Aaaaaaaahhh!!!" Ivey screamed to the top of her lungs.

"What's wrong? What happened?" Toni asked confused about whether the scream was excitement or agony.

"Girl! He proposed! I'm engaged! I'm getting married!" Ivey was close to hyperventilating.

"Calm down! You pregnant or something? Oh my bad, it ain't like you givin' him none. He can't even get that cat up out you, you sure he the one?" Toni said joking in only a way that she could.

"Why are you hating? I thought you would be happy for me. I knew it was too good to be true that you would actually act normal about this!" Ivey's voice was full of hurt.

"I'm not hating, I'm just playing devil's advocate." Toni retorted.

"Yeah, you're playing the devil alright. Thanks, but no thanks. What I need right now is a sister. I knew you were self-absorbed, but this is ridiculous. I would've gotten a better response from daddy! Thank you Toni for helping make this day special!" Ivey ranted right before she hung up on Toni.

Toni looked at the phone for a few seconds. She was so use to saying what she wanted to Ivey that Ivey's reaction took her by total surprise. She tried to call her back a few times to no avail. The comment about their dad hurt more than anything. Somehow Toni still found a way to make things about her.

"I'll buy her a make up gift." She said casually, not realizing the magnitude of the situation.

Ivey was really hurt. Since Ivey didn't have her mother to share in her excitement, she couldn't wait to tell her sister. She hadn't told anyone, not even her friends. So to get the reaction she did from her sister, hurt her and ruined what was supposed to be the happiest moment of her life.

Toni finally picked an outfit. Her head was messed up from the Ivey fiasco, so she got a shot of Courvoisier from the mini bar to put her head back in the game and get her loose for the video shoot.

She was well aware that her presence was going to cause a serious stir. These jobs were usually booked to capacity weeks in advance. So not only was she prepared to be in the video, she was aware that she would have to take someone's job to do it, even if it was Peaches and Red.

Toni pulled up to the video location in the heart of Hollywood. She was in awe of the atmosphere. Everyone seemed so absorbed in their own thing, like they all had a task of great importance. It made her feel like she was about her business, along with everyone else.

She approached the address of the shoot, she made a point to arrive early; this was not the place to be fashionably late. She wanted to be seen first, so she would be an automatic shoe in.

Toni grabbed her Coach duffle bag and powered down her IPhone. She didn't want any distractions. Wearing a black Dolce and Gabbana cat suit covered by a sheer and satin cover up that made a man want to see what was underneath, Toni entered the room and was instantly noticed. She saw that neither Peaches nor Red had arrived.

"What agency are you with?" Asked a cute, tall, blonde white girl that approached Toni with a clipboard.

"Affinity." Toni said without thinking twice.

The woman pointed her in the direction of a group of women across the room. As Toni approached the women she made note of all their flaws. "Ugly." "Bad weave." "Tacky." "No style." "No class." "Looks like a clown." After she took inventory, all she could think was, "These bitches need makeovers!"

Just then, Red and Peaches walked in looking almost as good as she did, she thought. But Toni didn't hate, she welcomed competition, even if she felt there was none.

"Long time no see." Toni said to Red as she delivered a feather light embrace. Toni still had yet to address Peaches. She decided she'd let her marinate on the fact that she had lied about her trip.

"Hey there, how'd you know about the video?" Red asked Toni with a look of confusion.

"I have my sources." Toni said, giving Peaches a look out of the corner of her eye. She finally addressed Peaches, as if she just realized she was present. "You're a long way from New York." Toni commented as she turned to walk away, not giving Peaches a chance to respond.

As if on cue, the producer walked up and hand-picked Toni for the lead video girl. Peaches and Red were also chosen, along with three other women. Toni could feel the heat coming from the sisters but she didn't care. As far as she was concerned, they were lucky to get a part at all.

Toni nailed her role as the lead and got the contact information for the video producer G. Styles. Things worked out better than she planned. Now she had the hook up and didn't need Red's assistance. It was on. They were her competitors at this point, and she intended to show them much better than she could tell them.

Pay to the Order of:

Showers were Toni's favorite form of relaxation. After the video shoot she jumped into the rainforest shower in her hotel suite. She stood and let the water run from her head to her toes, and it felt heavenly.

After her shower, she oiled her skin with Donna Karen Cashmere Mist lotion. She wanted to smell good enough to eat in her sheer red thong and Louboutin red bottom heels.

Toni poured a glass of Moscato and lay across the bed to await her visitor. She left a key for him at the front desk so she knew now all she had to do was wait. Her timing was perfect; she had only waited for a minute when she heard the key card slide into the door.

When the door opened Jojo couldn't help but to be pleasantly surprised when he saw her minimal attire. All of the guilt he felt about leaving the kids with a nanny and seeing Toni in general, just flew right out the window. He admired everything from the ponytail that lay across her shoulder down to the sexy pumps she sported. He was sure not to miss her plump naked breasts as well.

She had to admit that Jojo was also looking sexy in all of his ghetto glory. He wore a wife beater with Polo jeans and a Louis Vutton belts and boots, simple and sexy.

"You ready to cash this check?" Toni asked in a low seductive voice.

"Hell yeah, cash it, flip it, rub it down." Jo said seriously, but Toni couldn't help but laugh.

"Pour you a drink." Toni said pointing him in the direction of the bar. She already had Hennessy Privilege waiting.

Jojo poured him a drink and took out an already rolled cush blunt. He made the necessary preparations by putting a wet towel under the room door. Then he picked up his drink and his blunt and made his way to the bed next to Toni.

"Take that shit off." Toni commanded referring to his shoes and clothes.

His nature rose as she spoke. He was completely turned on by her aggressive behavior. It made him want her more.

"You take it off." He told her with an equal sense of command in his voice.

Toni put her glass of wine on the night stand and crawled up to Jojo. She took his drink and sat it next to hers. Then she took the blunt and placed it between her lips.

"Gimme a light." Toni requested.

He lit the blunt and watched as she French inhaled the smoke through her nose then she placed her lips on his and blew the smoke into his mouth. She pulled his shirt over his head as she purposely placed her bare breast in his face.

He grabbed them and hungrily sucked in both nipples at once. Toni sighed with pleasure as Jojo took one hand and gently caressed her clit that was already swollen from her arousal. She handed him the still burning blunt and crawled between his legs where she unbuckled and unbuttoned his pants.

Taking the head of his penis in her mouth, she slowly pulled his jeans down his thighs. He tried to smoke but her actions made it difficult. Once she removed his pants and shoes, his fully erect penis was exposed to the elements. She returned to her knees in front of him and slowly licked his inner thigh from his gunshot wound to his nuts.

"Oh shit!" Jojo was in total bliss.

That area of his body was extremely sensitive and only Toni knew it. When she made it to his pulsating prize, she licked and sucked him into oblivion. Jojo couldn't wait to taste her and was even more excited about feeling the wetness of her juices flowing from her tight pussy.

He was on the verge of exploding when he grabbed her head to stop her. She stood up and straddled his lap while taking and relighting the blunt. She blew the smoke into his mouth again as she began to grind on him making her even wetter.

"Put that pussy on my face." Jo instructed Toni as he caressed her full round ass.

She happily obliged him and crawled up to his face planting her juices on his lips.

"Mmmm." Jo moaned as he sucked her clit and teased it with his tongue simultaneously. Now he made it difficult for her to smoke. Her passionate sexy moans made his already hard dick get harder. He slid on a Magnum while Toni rode his face.

"Now put that pussy on this dick." He said muffled by Toni's muff.

But she understood every word and in one motion lifted her body from his face and slid down to his shaft. They both moaned with pleasure. Toni handed him the barely lit blunt and worked her hips while she sat up and they watched each other.

He watched as she threw her head back and tried to regain her composure while he met her with passionate thrusts. And Toni watched Jojo try to smoke as she rode him and played with his nipples.

Then as if he couldn't take another second, he put the weed in the ashtray and flipped Toni on her back never removing himself from her wet walls. He gave her long slow strokes until he could see that she was at the peak of an orgasm. He gradually sped up the pace and hardened his thrust until they released together.

After five minutes of panting and sweating, Toni said out of the blue, "Okay, it's time for you to go."

Jojo knew not to argue it was just her way of doing things. So he got up, got dressed, and got out. He was on his way back to the airport then to Atlanta to spend time with Raina and Ryan.

When he left, Toni prepared to take another shower. She sat on the edge of the bed and lit the blunt Jojo left. After she took a long drag, she released the smoke and said to herself. "Why does something so wrong have to be so damn good."

In Shambles

Ivey was more upset with her sister than she had ever been. But after not answering Toni's calls for two days, Ivey decided it was time to hear what she had to say. After continuous unanswered calls to Toni, Ivey decided to stop by her loft. Toni was so secretive about her whereabouts, that Ivey wasn't even aware that she was in Los Angeles.

As Ivey walked up to Toni's door, she noticed the door was already ajar about an inch. She figured maybe Toni hadn't closed the door completely. When she walked into the apartment to Toni's belongings tossed all over the place, she attempted to quietly search to make sure Toni wasn't hurt.

As she made her way into the living room area, she noticed a DVD and a set of photos sitting on the ottoman. The photos were of Toni with a man and a woman in lewd sexual positions. Ivey was in shock as she shuffled through each picture. They got more explicit the more she looked. Ivey eventually dropped the pictures and grabbed her cell. This time she text Toni. "911!" was all the text read. This assured her that whatever Toni was involved in at the time, took no precedence over returning the call. They both agreed not to send that text unless it was an absolute emergency. So no matter what they were doing at the time had to wait.

Toni was awakened by the text. When she saw it, she jumped up from her king sized hotel bed and immediately called Ivey.

"What's wrong?" Toni asked before giving Ivey a chance to say, hello.

"Someone broke into your place and left some.....well shall I say incriminating evidence. Plus they trashed everything. Where are you anyway?" Ivey managed to get out all in one breath.

"Well first of all, I'll be home today, never mind where I am. And what kind of incriminating evidence are you talking about?" Toni was extremely aggravated.

"There are picture of you and several people in various sexual positions. There is also a DVD that I'm actually afraid to look at." Ivey admitted.

"Is there anything missing?" Toni asked before giving her next instructions to Ivey.

"I don't know, I can't really tell, but it doesn't seem like it. It looks more trashed that anything.

"Okay, no police. I'll be home in a few hours. Just get out of there and lock the door." Toni had done so much over the years, she was afraid to rely on the help of the police for fear of her own incarceration. Ivey was confused about what was going on but reluctantly she followed her sister's orders, and left the loft.

When in Rome

When Toni returned to St. Louis, she went to her loft to assess the damages. She didn't want to admit to Ivey that the pictures and DVD were already in her apartment. There wasn't anything missing, but for her safety she decided it best that she stay somewhere else for the time being. Just a few weeks at the most, she figured.

Although she and Ivey still had tension, Ivey insisted that Toni stayed with her until she figured things out. Ivey had a two bedroom condo, so there was plenty of room for the both of them. Romero had Toni's loft paid up for the year, so that was one less thing she had to worry about.

Rome actually suggested that she move to Atlanta where he could protect her. Of course, that wasn't his only motivation for wanting her close, but it was the most important reason at the time. She was not looking to be tied down or kept track of, but she knew moving to where Rome was, would mean exactly that.

It was early Sunday morning, and Toni was awakened by the smell of breakfast: Sage sausage, maple bacon, eggs, and pancakes, to be exact. She had only been at Ivey's for a few days, so she was still getting use to the early morning movement. She moved around the room slowly trying to get her bearings. She slipped into her Victoria's Secrets robe and slippers and made her way down to the kitchen.

Brandon sat at the table watching Ivey put the finishing touches on breakfast. Toni quietly observed the way Brandon looked at Ivey; it was like she had a spell over him. His eyes illuminated with the love he felt for her, and Toni could see it. She wondered how her sister managed to get a man to love her that way, and if she would ever find the kind of love Ivey and Brandon shared.

"Good morning." Ivey said interrupting Toni's thoughts.

"Hey yall." Toni sounded exhausted.

"Hey." Brandon said dryly.
He was not happy about Toni's reaction to their engagement. In fact, Toni still had yet to congratulate either of them.

"So, do you come over at the crack of dawn every morning?" Toni asked Brandon, knowing full well that Ivey hadn't allowed him to spend the night. Ivey cut her eyes at Toni, because she was aware of what she was implying.

"As a matter of fact," Ivey started before Brandon could respond. "We're going to church. You're already awake, so you should get some of this coffee, eat, and get dressed. You might actually enjoy yourself." She said.

"Or catch fire." Brandon whispered under his breath. Ivey walked by and gently nudged him in the back of the head with her elbow.

"Church? Girl please, that's yo thing, Mother Theresa." Toni said stealing a piece of bacon off the plate in the middle of the table.

"Well, we're announcing our engagement to the congregation today. It would be really nice to have my actual family present when we do." Ivey shot Toni a look that could only spell one thing.....guilt trip.

The church that they attended, God's Kingdom, was pastored by Brandon's father, Rev. Earnest Cameron. So, Ivey spent a lot of time with and around the Camerons. Ivey and Toni's parents were both from the south, so any other relatives they had were distant in relation and miles. They were literally all they had.

Toni reluctantly found something appropriate to wear to church then climbed in the back seat of Brandon's Impala. Her hair was in a messy ponytail and she wore a pair of black slacks with a navy wrap around silk blouse. She also wore some simple slide on mules with a low heal, no designers. "I'm not wasting my good clothes on church." She thought to herself. Yet and still her makeup was flawless.

Getting Toni to sit in the front of the church was like pulling teeth. Ivey was finally able to convince her that she wanted them all together when she made the announcement.

One of the younger Deacons stood to take the pulpit. He was delivering the message this Sunday. Deacon David James was the youngest on the Deacon board, but was noted by the Pastor to be one of the most promising at only twenty four years old.

Toni paid attention to nothing about the service until Deacon James stood in front of the congregation. He had an undeniable quiet power about himself. Tall, dark, and handsome described him to a tee. And he wore a navy three pieced suit that made him look as distinguished as the President himself.

Toni sat up in her seat and tried to appear attentive. She tried to find the passage he instructed the church to turn to in the bible she retrieved from the bench she now occupied.

"Hosea ten and twelve says, Sow to yourself in righteousness, reap in mercy; break up your fallow ground: for it is time to seek the Lord, till he come and rain righteousness upon you!" The Deacon bellowed. "Let's take a minute to analyze the word fallow. Fallow is the condition or period of being unseeded and unseeded ground will not produce fruit. See, what we must understand church, is that we must sow the seed of righteousness in order to reap or return our mercy from God. The mercy of the blood of Jesus, by the power of

God, gives us a second chance to make a first impression. God forgives! He doesn't dismiss us like we do one another, His love is unconditional. The Lord shows us mercy like no other parent in the world...."

The Deacon continued his sermon as Toni nudged Ivey's arm and whispered. "I wanna meet him." Ivey didn't comment, she decided to let this play out on its own. Most of the young women in the church wanted a piece of Deacon James, but he was completely focused on his ministry. He and Brandon spoke often about him and Ivey's relationship and the Deacon made it abundantly clear that he would marry when God gave him permission. He was convicted about his mission.

After the service, Toni grabbed Ivey's arm and made a beeline to the Deacon. As they got close Toni admired how handsome he was. He was about six foot six inches tall and his college football physique could not be hidden through his suit. As they approached him, his full lips parted to expose the most perfect white teeth Toni had ever seen on a man. She admired how his perfectly trimmed mustache seemed to melt into his chocolate skin and how well groomed he was with his cold black waves.

"Beautiful." Toni said under her breath, not even realizing she had spoken aloud.

"Hello Deacon James, your service was enlightening." Ivey said shaking hands with the Deacon.

"Thank you and congratulations on your engagement." Deacon James embraced Ivey.

"I'd like you to meet my sister, Antoinette Danes." She motioned toward Toni. "Toni, Deacon James."

"I enjoyed your message Deacon." Toni puts on her shy, sexy alter ego.

"Thank you so much Ms. Danes. It's a pleasure to meet you." The Deacon firmly shook her hand then moved on.

Ivey watched as Toni's expression changed instantly to sheer confusion. He had to be the first man to encounter her face to face and not take obvious notice of her beauty.

However, the sermon actually resonated with her. He was physically enchanting, but something about his conviction made her want to know him. He was completely nothing like the men she usually dealt with and even she had a hard time understanding how she felt. But the one thing she did know is that she was going to be attending church a little more often.

Red Alert

Peaches and Red flew back to New York after they finished the shoot in LA. Peaches decided she would spend about a week with her little sister before Jojo returned to St. Louis with her children.

Red had exhausted every resource trying to find out how Toni infiltrated the video shoot. No one knew or could explain how Toni got access to the privileged information. She let it go for now, but she knew the last thing she needed was competition from Toni. She wasn't jealous, but she wasn't stupid either. She had eyes and could see how beautiful Toni was, just as much as the next person. So when she realized Toni was a threat, she thought, "Why am I bringing my own competition?" With that thought, Toni was never invited to another job with them again.

Peaches felt bad about leaving her out of the loop. She had considered Toni a friend. Red and Toni however, had grown apart long ago and Red only dealt with her because of Peaches. So Red had no residual feelings because of her actions.

"Find anything out?" Peaches asked Red referring to Toni showing up in California.

"Nope, still nothing. But she better be careful dealing with ole boy." Red warned.

"Who, the producer, um what's his name, G Styles?" Peaches inquired.

"Yeah, the nigga's grimy. If you don't have an agent, he'll try to fuck you sideways, literally." Red added.

Red wasn't a huge fan of Toni's but she figured she would tell Peaches so she can warn her friend if she sees fit to do so.

"How are my niece and nephew?" Red asked changing the subject.

"Girl, they alright. Shhhhhh! They might mess around and knock on your door." Peaches joked. They both laughed.

Red knew her sister was not the maternal type, so she was glad to see that Peaches was even partially parental. It seemed that everyone except the children knew that Jojo wasn't their father, but he was the better parent between the two. And she was grateful, because that meant she would have to become someone's parent or guardian prematurely.

Peaches had been dealing with Jojo on and off since high school. They were familiar with each other plus, they never stopped sleeping together. So, when she had babies, they just "made it do what it do" in Peaches' words.

Red moved to New York immediately after she graduated high school at age seventeen. And although her behavior caused her to have to spend a majority of her teens in children's homes, she was actually exceptionally intelligent. She received a full academic scholarship to NYU. Red fell in love with New York and hadn't looked back. She visited her parents from time to time, but their relationship was scarce. Her main connection to St. Louis, were her sister and her niece and nephew.

"I got information about another video. This time there will be a photo shoot for all the models as well." Red informed Peaches.

"Aw yeah? When, where, and how?" Peaches asked.

"It's actually in two weeks, in Atlanta. But I'm not crazy about Atlanta, so I usually just fly out the day of and come right back to New York." Red said as more of a suggestion than anything.

"You trippin', The ATL is hot! I know I kick it every time Jo fly me out there." Peaches told Red with complete and total disagreement. "Actually the most fun I had out of town was in Atlanta. You must be rolling with the wrong people." She added.

"I don't "roll" with anyone." Red said rolling her eyes while doing finger quotations. Red didn't do cliques or chicks, it was her motto. She was a loner and she preferred it that way.

"Okay, well I'm your sister, so I think you can make an exception in this case. We're staying for two days." Peaches said matter of factly, while holding up the peace sign to indicate the number two. She wanted to be clear. "We gone kick it with Jo and Rome, that way we won't have to pay for shit." Peaches smiled at her idea, she had it all figured out.

"Um, what's a Rome?" Red asked.

"Romero Wallace, that's Jojo's business partner. They moved down to Atlanta together after the Feds was trippin' with Jojo in St. Louis. I told you this! You make me sick acting like ain't nobody's life important but yours." Peaches caught an instant attitude.

"Look, I don't do ghetto shit. And besides, if the Feds weren't after you, I don't give a damn about much else! Anyway, I'll hang with you and your people in Atlanta for a couple of days." Red told Peaches, not at all excited.

"I'd better not regret this shit!" She told Peaches. But her true concern was whether or not Toni's "sources" as she so eloquently put it, would bring them face to face again with their rival frienemy.

Reflections

Toni sat up in bed in Ivey's guestroom thinking about what she heard at church a few days before. The words "forgiveness" "love" and "repent" kept playing over and over in her head. She knew a lot of "church folk" so she called them and none of them had lived their lives like she had, as far as she had known. So when she sat and thought about all the things she would need to be forgiven for, she knew those words couldn't apply to her.

She had never really evaluated her own actions, because until now, she didn't see anything wrong with them. In her young life, Toni had experienced things that the average person would never experience. She was never abused or molested. Her experiences were actually self-inflicted. Drugs, alcohol, multiple group sexual escapades, the list could've went on and on. And even though she seemed to take him for granted, she was actually happy to have something as consistent as Romero in her life.

Although they were not a couple like he wanted, Romero accepted her for who she was and he still took care of her. They were sure to contact one another at least once every day, in some form or another. Rome was uncomfortable about leaving her in St. Louis, but he also didn't have a choice in the matter. So he took care of her from afar the best he could. Even Toni was unaware of how closely he kept watch over her.

Toni thumbed through the explicit photos that Ivey took from her apartment. She already knew what was on the video, but she didn't understand its importance to whoever broke in her place. The video was a threesome between herself and the couple in the pictures, Lisa and Larry, or so they called themselves. She met them at PT's strip club in Centerville, IL on swinger's night.

PT's

Toni walked through the strip club and was the center of attention. She had already reserved a spot on the stage/dance floor. That's where all of the action took place. As she sashayed through the club, random men reached for her hands and random women grabbed her ass. She was on the menu as she returned to her spot on the stage. She sat on a plush leather chair watching the action unfolding on the dance floor.

There were several black leather love seats and chairs strategically placed. The lighting was dim. Light enough to see once you focused your eyes and dark enough to make a person comfortable about their indiscretions.

Her eyes examined the inventory in front of her when she noticed a beautiful woman admiring her while she masturbated with her anatomy fully exposed to Toni.

Toni's eyes locked with hers as she admired the woman's plump round breast and clean shaven vagina. Toni licked her lips slowly and deliberately, almost as if she could taste the woman from across the floor.

The woman looked to be of Latin decent. She had jet black hair that hung in long layers down her back. She had a petite shapely frame. "Sexy." Toni whispered just as a fine man that appeared to be of the same nationality, walked up to the woman and tapped her lips with his hard penis. Toni's clit began to throb at the sight of the Latino goddess giving oral pleasure like it was her profession. Not to mention, the woman never took her eyes off of Toni.

She observed the tall olive complected gentleman also staring in her direction. His eyes were green and pierced right through her. She wanted them both.

When Toni went out on her sexcapades, she always wore red. It made her feel nasty. So tonight she wore a red mini dress with red crotch less fishnet stockings. The couple approached her after the woman orgasmed with the man's manhood still down her throat.

"You're even more beautiful up close." The woman said with a Spanish accent.

Toni felt the same way when she saw how attractive the exotic Latina actually was. But there was no time for compliments. Toni needed to make sure this couple was freaky enough to satisfy her fetish. By this time, Toni was *touching her own womanhood with her dress waist high, no underwear in sight.*

"Get down on your knees and taste it." Toni commanded, speaking directly to the woman. "And I want him", Toni motioned her head in the man's direction. "To fuck you while you're doing it.

Within seconds, she was on her knees with her head between Toni's thighs. While she ate, the man continued with Toni's demands and penetrated the sexy vixen from behind. They were perfect. She loved to dominate and they followed orders well.

They left the club and went to the couple's hotel room at the Four Seasons in downtown St. Louis. That's where they gave the names Lisa and Larry. Her first thought was, "Yeah right, more like Lupe and Lorenzo." But it didn't matter because she never gave her real name either. As far as they knew her name was Nina. They revealed that they were in town on business and lived in Brazil. "No wonder they're so beautiful." She thought. Then she allowed the couple to record their pornographic experience. There was no exchange of personal information between Toni and the couple, except for the email address Toni gave them to forward her a copy of their indiscretions. After the things she demanded of the couple that night, they will never forget St. Louis, and they would definitely never forget Nina.

That encounter happened almost three years ago and she had never heard from "Lisa" and "Larry" since. Toni began to think back over the events of the past week. She runs into crazy ass Coco. Her apartment is trashed. The blue Mercedes truck and not to mention the private hang up phone calls she had been receiving lately.

Romero had always taught her to watch her back and she kept protection at all times. But she had to find out what was going on. Toni was about having control at all times. And one thing you can't control, is surprise. And Toni hated surprises.

Georgia on My Mind

Jojo pulled up to the Atlanta airport to pick up Red and Peaches. Their video and photo shoot wasn't for a few hours, which gave them time to relax from the trip and freshen up for the job at hand.

Red hadn't seen Mr. Grant for a few weeks and he was feigning. He planned to meet her in Atlanta and rendezvous after she finished working. Between traveling himself and sending her all over the country, they were hardly in the same place at the same time. So he always made a way to meet her somewhere in the middle to get his fix.

He reserved a suite at the St. Regis Atlanta Hotel. As usual, he sent her a text with the arrangements and she replied with confirmation that she would be available. He always bought her expensive jewelry or lingerie and had it delivered to the room in advance. This time it was a six carat white gold diamond tennis bracelet he knew she would love. He spared no expense when it came to

Red. She always expected a gift but considered herself classy enough to act completely surprised every time.

In the meantime, Red and Peaches prepared for the video and photo shoot with an upcoming artist being signed by Grand Hustle. No one knew who he was yet, so Red couldn't even remember his name. All she knew is they were spending a lot of money to promote him so he had to be predicted to be the next best thing.

When the women arrived at Jojo's house, Red couldn't help but to admire the beauty of the home. It was clearly a bachelor pad with the black and neutral colored décor. The house was immaculate. Jojo and Romero lived in a gated community. The four bedroom four and a half bath mini mansion was a total surprise to Red. She wasn't sure what to expect, but it wasn't this. There was a lagoon style pool in the backyard that was separate from the playground area Jojo had built for his children with Peaches. The house resembled something off of Cribs with its marble fireplace, high ceilings, and spiral staircase.

She still couldn't understand why Peaches stayed in a section 8 apartment in St. Louis, when she could've been living in luxury. Red shook her head at the thought. Red could never understand why Peaches was always drawn to the more hood aspects of life, because she always wanted so much more.

After Red hugged, kissed, and played with Raina and Ryan, she got her mind right for the task at hand. Red and her sister fit together like two puzzle pieces when it came to the video vixen game. Physically, Peaches had everything Red didn't and vice versa. However, Red felt she had one thing that made her a cut above the rest, no matter how attractive they were, and that's class.

Class allowed Red to move in any circle she wanted and fit in as if she was bread to be in attendance. She knew what to do and when. This made her a valuable asset, because it allowed her more opportunities than most in her position.

Red shook off the slight anxiety she felt at the thought of Toni showing up in Atlanta. She focused her mind and practiced her sexiest moves and poses in the full length mirror of the master bathroom.

She loved everything about this house including the skylight in the bathroom that she admired as her phone alerted her to a text message. "1501" Was all that the message from Mr. Grant read. It was the number to the Penthouse suite at the St. Regis Hotel.

She entered the master bedroom to continue getting ready. She hadn't noticed when she entered, how masculine and sheik the room was. It resembled a room that represented a catalog for rich bachelors. The mahogany furniture with leather finishing was traditional but sexy all at the same time.

As Red sat on the corner of the chocolate leather chaise lounger, oiling her body, she hoped Peaches was getting dressed instead of getting dicked down by Jojo. She hardly noticed when the bedroom door opened. But when she did, she was not at all prepared for what entered the doorway.

Looks had never been important to her because they came a dime a dozen and didn't amount to anything without money. Romero however, was something altogether different. She couldn't believe her own body's reaction to this man. But she never let him see her sweat.

"I'm sorry, I wasn't aware I had company." Romero joked, referring to her being in his bedroom.

"Romero, I take it?" She asked extending her hand to greet him. All she wore was a camisole and a thong, but she interacted with him like she was fully dressed. "I'm Red, Peaches sister. Jo told me I could use this room to get dressed. I can relocate if you have somewhere else I can change." Red said not wanting to invade his space or wear out her welcome.

"Naw, you good Mah." She barely heard him say while taking him all in. He wore a black wife beater and black Polo jeans. His body was lean and chiseled and secretly whispered, "Come fuck me" to Red.

She shook off the thought as she snapped back into reality. When she did, she noticed that Romero was caught up in a tattoo she had received a few weeks prior. It was a trail of butterflies that went from her ankle to her ass cheek. She wanted to step up her look for the video game and she wanted to surprise Mr. Grant.

"Um um." She cleared her throat. "Some privacy please?" She almost didn't mean it.

"I'm sorry baby, take your time. I found what I was looking for." He said holding up a black cd case.

He stepped out of the room and closed the door behind him. All Red could say was "DAMN! Peaches could've at least warned me he was that fine." Of course she knew that kind of information wasn't shared with her because Peaches knew those kinds of things were irrelevant to Red, until today.

Romero went into his den and placed a Scarface cd in the cd player. He sent a quick text to Toni to make sure all was well with her. Just as he hit "send", his mind floated back to Red.

She was physically not his type, but she intrigued him. He wasn't even sure what it was and it baffled him. To look at her on the surface, she was "aight" as far as looks were concerned. But he felt there was so much more to her, and he could tell from their short interaction. He received Toni's response that everything was okay and his mind was at ease about her safety.

He had already made plans for the girls for the weekend, at Jojo's request. Rome couldn't get Red out of his head, but he couldn't forget that Peaches and Toni were friends. And although Toni refused to commit, he didn't want to ruffle any feathers. So he made up his mind. "I will show them a good time, and that's it." He said out loud before pouring a glass of Hennessy Privilege.

The video shoot was crazy when Red and Peaches arrived. There were twice the women than there was at the shoot in LA, which meant twice the competition. Red was relieved when Toni didn't show, but they still had to be on top of their game.

The two sisters earned their spot in the video. They were in the middle of the photo shoot when Red heard "Sugar Daddy's Girl" by Lauren Mayhew, coming from her phone letting her know the Mr. Grant was trying to reach her. After the photo shoot she sent a quick "still working" text.

When the girls were done, Jojo picked them up and took them back to the house to get ready for the night at hand. Both women made sure they would be in the top ten wherever they went. They were both dressed to the teeth and their makeup was fabulous.

They both wore body fitting BeBe dresses. Red in white and Peaches in black. They were and have always been yin and yang. The foursome walked into Club Vision and the atmosphere was hot.

Red had to admit that she was actually enjoying herself, the music, the drinks, and even Romero. She tried to ignore the effect he was having on her. He made sure to keep his distance and eye contact all at the same time. He was attracted to Red and didn't even want to be.

As "Drunk in Love" by Beyonce played, they made eye contact with one another. Rome slowly walked towards her without breaking his stare. He approached her just as "We be all night!" blasted through the speakers and Romero put his leg between Red's thighs to ignite the dirty dancing that commenced next.

They danced like they had known each other forever. When the night was over, they all rode in the back of a Lincoln Limousine back to Jo and Rome's house.

Red instinctively went back to the room where she originally got dressed and that held all her belongings.

"We meet here again?" Rome said walking into the bedroom while Red ruffled through her suitcase. By this time it was three a.m. and everyone was winding down.

"I'm just getting my things. Can you point me in the direction of an unoccupied room? She asked.

"You can stay here. You a guest and it's plenty of room. Get comfortable, I'll sleep somewhere else." He insisted.

She had watched him all night. He was even more handsome than their original meeting. He cleaned up well, but she was not at all surprised. Even though he was considered a hood dude, he dressed like he was the CEO of a fortune 500 company, suit, tie, and dress shoes. He camouflaged well.

"Thank you." She said as she walked up to Romero and planted a kiss on his face as close to his mouth as she could get without kissing his lips. Almost instantaneously, he grabbed her around the waist and kissed her passionately. He couldn't help himself.

He let her go. "I apologize, I shouldn't have done that."

"Then that means I shouldn't do this?" Red grabbed Rome by the back of his head and kissed him like she belonged to him.

He instinctively grabbed her thighs and lifted her to match his height. She wrapped her legs around his waist and he grabbed her small ass with his massive hands.

Rome had also watched her that night. He imagined ravaging her when they got back to the house, but that was only a thought. He didn't imagine that he would actually be holding her in his arms at that moment. He gently lay her on his king sized bed and removed every piece of her clothing as gently as a mother undressing her newborn baby. All the while, their eye contact was never broken. They both actually found out what making love was that night.

The sun started to shine through a small crack in the blinds as Red heard her phone go off for the twentieth time or so. All she could think was, "I'm so sorry Mr. Grant."

A Precious Gift

(Eight years ago)

"Momma, how will I know when I'm ready for a boyfriend?" Asked a curious thirteen year old Ivey.

"When I tell you you're ready." Lois responded with a look of concern.

"Is there a boy you like?" Lois tried to sound like this line of questioning didn't scare the hell out of her. She put the top on the jambalaya she was preparing and turned to face Ivey. Then, she leaned against the stove, just in case the conversation caused her to lose her balance.

"No, but everybody got a boyfriend so I was just wondering." Ivey wasn't in a hurry, she just figured it was part of growing up.

"What do you mean everybody? Toni's not allowed to have a boyfriend." Lois looked at Ivey from the corner of her eyes.

"I meant everybody else." Ivey tried to cover up for her already sexually active big sister.

"Mmm Hmm. Well, just so you know, a boyfriend is not important right now. You should be focused on school, God, and becoming a respectable young lady. Ivey at this age, boys don't hold your best interest at heart. They say what sounds good so they can take the most precious gift you have, your innocence. Boys aren't going anywhere, but once you lose your innocence and your teenage years, you can't get them back. You may not want to hear this but technically, you shouldn't be worried about a boyfriend until you're ready to settle down and get married. God wants you to remain pure. And if you give your body to someone, it should be your husband. I know it sounds like a long time to wait, but when you're obedient you get God's blessings." Lois preached.

Ivey listened to her mother. The things Lois said resonated with her. She continued on about trust and having respect for you. She took the time to discuss the same topic with Toni, but it was obvious to her from the difference in the girl's reactions, that these values would mean a lot more to Ivey than they would to Toni.

Present day

Ivey had managed to keep her virtue in tact up until this point. She knew her mother would be proud that she saved herself for her husband. The thought of a wedding without her mother saddened her.

She snapped out of her sadness when she thought of the task at hand. She was getting ready to attend a youth program she volunteered for to help teen girls. Today's event focused on self-respect and preserving innocence until marriage. Ivey figured if she could do it, that she could be an example to the teens that felt it was impossible to wait. To her, it was a badge of honor to be able to say she was still a virgin at age twenty one. She was proud of herself, but she was even more proud of Brandon for waiting.

He, on the other hand, was not a virgin. But he loved Ivey so much that he wouldn't take her virginity before they got married, even if she tried to give it to him. He cherished the fact that he would be her first and only. Brandon was also part of the program and supported her every step of the way. Ivey finally convinced Toni to attend. She figured the continuous begging helped a little.

Toni hadn't gone back to church since she first moved in, but what she heard that day never left her. Between traveling in and out of town, she went clubbing more frequently to rebel against the feeling in her gut telling her there was more to life than what she was getting. Ivey wasn't even aware of how the sermon affected Toni that day.

Today was bitter sweet for Ivey as she prepared to do a poem by one of the girls she once mentored.

"I welcome you all to enjoy our program today. I would like to start with a poem by one of my girls." Ivey stated to begin the program.

"I can't get you back

I said goodbye for the first and last time when I gave you away.
You were so precious to me but I didn't allow you to stay.

You begged to stay with me cause if I let you go you'd cease to exist.
I should have made you top priority on my list.

But I knocked you down the list a peg or two,
When I dealt with those that did not value you.

An apology cannot change the outcome of your fate.
I abandoned you and now it's too late.

I have not been the same since I gave you to him.
He won't give you back now our future looks dim.

I wish now I had allowed our relationship to grow.
I would've valued you more and told that boy, NO!

Now he's got you and so many others he can't keep track.
I cry out to my virginity, and I can't get you back."

Ivey continued. "This poem is very dear to my heart for many reasons. As most of you know, I myself have chosen to save myself for marriage. But more importantly, Mia, the young lady that wrote this poem came to me as a mentee when she was four months pregnant, at fifteen years old. It was her first and last sexual encounter. This beautiful young lady died giving birth to her stillborn daughter. When I think back to how she regretted her decision to have sex, I also think about the fact that she never thought the consequence would have been her life. Today's society urges young people to protect themselves. Well today, I am urging young people to preserve themselves, thank you."

The members of the audience erupted in applause and those that knew the young poet, were in tears. Ivey brought a powerful message that day, which she prayed made a difference in their lives.

Toni was impressed by the program her little sister put together. She admired Ivey for many reasons that she was just realizing for the first time. She admired her strength for putting up with her for so long. She admired Ivey's discipline in pursuing her education and remaining a virgin. She also admired her spirituality. Toni had to admit it to herself, but Ivey was actually stronger than she was. But she would only admit it to herself.

"Hello Ms. Danes." Toni heard a familiar voice say as she looked up at Deacon James. "I've missed you at church the past few weeks, how have you been?" He asked seemingly with genuine concern for her.

Toni was surprised that he even remembered her after the way he dismissed her when they were first introduced.

"Hello Deacon. I'm hanging in there." She said.

"Will I see you on Sunday?" He asked her.

"Maybe." She smiled, but wondered about his sudden interest and friendliness.

"Well I hope to see you here." He smiled as he walked to greet the other church members.

Toni watched him, admiring his handsome smile and perfect teeth. She felt slight shame in the fact that a fine man was the only way God could get her to attend church. "I should be ashamed of myself." Toni said under her breath as she got her outfit for Sunday together in her head. "Something modest, but sexy." She thought.

Sunday

Toni got up early Sunday morning. She put on a navy two piece Donna Karen pencil skirt suit. She was awake before Ivey so she put on a pot of coffee. She thought about cooking breakfast, but decided against it. She didn't want to smell like food when they arrived at church.

When Ivey entered the kitchen, she was startled when she noticed Toni at the kitchen table, already dressed.

"Girl, you scared the mess outta me! You just get in?" Ivey asked her knowing she wasn't up and dressed for church already.

"No heffa! I'm ready for church." Toni said rolling her eyes at Ivey.

"And to what do I owe this honor?" Ivey asked while pouring a cup of coffee.

"Um, earth to Ivey. My going to church is not about you or for you, for that matter. I'm tryna um, get some religion." Toni lied.

"You tryna get some alright, but it ain't got nothing to do with religion. But you keep barking up that tree and you'll get a lot more than you bargained for." She teased Toni.

"What is that supposed to mean?" Toni asked.

"It means, while you're trying to corrupt Deacon James, you may be surprised at what forces are more powerful. And I'm a leave you with that." Ivey said as she headed upstairs with her cup of coffee to get dressed.

"Whatever, I get what I want." Toni mumbled under her breath.

Church

"Please turn to Jonah two and eight. They that observe lying vanities forsake their own mercy. Let's ponder that for a moment church. Lying vanities. We endure countless lying vanities on a daily basis, money, sex, music, and even the media. The media makes what God has made clear to his children as "lying vanities", okay in every day society. And we allow these demons to infiltrate our thinking, to accept these things as right. This thinking, in turn, tricks us into forsaking our own mercy, like the children of Israel did when they served Baal instead of the Lord. It's like allowing a con man to trick you out of your life savings! God has promised us forgiveness and mercy. Don't allow Satan and his lying vanities to steal your inheritance." Deacon James whaled his sermon to the congregation.

"Amen!" The crowd replied in unison.

Toni tried to imagine the things she would do to this man once she seduced him. But she couldn't ignore the message in his sermon that seemed to be directed at her.

After the services, Toni remained seated on the bench in the second row, watching as the Deacon approached where she was seated as he greeted the members of the church, including Brandon and Ivey.

"Ms. Danes." The Deacon nodded toward Toni as he greeted her with a firm handshake.

"I really enjoyed your message Deacon. I'm trying to explore my spirituality and I am still getting clarity on some things. Is it possible for us to do lunch?" Toni said as she discretely put her phone number in his hand. She smiled and walked away without waiting for a response.

"Your move Deacon." Toni said to herself as she exited the church doors.

Skeletons

Jojo escorted Peaches and the children back to St. Louis and decided to stay for a couple of weeks. He stayed with Peaches while he was in town so he could spend as much time around the children as possible. Jo figured it was cool since he and Peaches had no problems co-existing, plus he had "in-house". And when he wanted, he could have "out-house", no questions.

The clock on the night stand read 5:42 am and Jojo could feel Peaches fondling his manhood. Then he felt the warmth of her mouth engulf his penis.

"Damn Toni." Jojo moaned with pleasure.

"What the fuck you just call me?" Peaches screamed, abruptly interrupting his morning blow job.

"Whatchu talkin' about Peaches?" He asked not even realizing what he just said.

"You fucking that bitch! Don't lie nigga! I knew it!" Peaches accused.

"Fucking who? Calm yo ass down girl!" Jojo roared. Apparently she had forgotten who she was talking to.

"Nigga you called me Toni." Peaches said through clenched teeth.

"Girl you trippin', I ain't said no shit like that! Man you fucking up the vibe in here with that bull shit." Jo said as he got out of bed. Peaches followed in hot pursuit. She was right on his tail when he entered the kitchen.

"You think I'm stupid. That would explain so much, like how you keep finding out all my business and......" Peaches gasped as she realized how far the information highway may have gone. "You told her about the video shoot in LA!" It was like every unexplained incident just came to fruition in an instant.

Whap! "Girl what the fuck?" He turned suddenly and grabbed Peaches by the wrists. Jo didn't believe in hitting women, but she had one more swing before she felt his wrath. Peaches was screaming and swinging, and that combination was about to push him over the edge, no matter how wrong he was.

"I'm a tell you this one more time, calm yo ass down!" He yelled still holding her wrists.

By that time, she was out of breath with tears streaming down her face. Peaches knew she and Jojo weren't an official item, but he and Toni crossed the line. She snatched away from him with a look of pure rage in her eyes. Even though he never verbally admitted it; she knew he had been with Toni.

"This shit is fucked up." She scowled before turning to walk away.

"You didn't seem to feel that way about Red fucking Rome, hypocrite." Jo said as he continued to roll his morning blunt.

He was right and Peaches knew it. She knew the true nature of her and Jo's relationship, but she never thought that Toni's competitive side went this far. She needed to talk to Red. She wanted to make sure that Romero fell as deeply in love with Red as Romeo did Juliet. She knew then that Toni would be cut off. Cut off from Rome, Rome's family, Rome's money, and most importantly Rome's protection.

Lunch Guests

To Toni's surprise Deacon James had in fact called to do lunch. He told her he was "lead" to sit down and talk with her about any confusion she had. They decided to meet at St. Louis Italian Restaurant.

The restaurant was on DeBalivere which was near Central West End, so she decided to check on her apartment before meeting the Deacon. She had gone by about a week or two prior to clean up the mess left by the anonymous intruder. She was still getting strange phone calls, but she was okay as long as they were only calls. She figured she would get around to changing her number eventually.

As she pulled away from the Metro Loft building to head to the restaurant, she noticed the blue Mercedes truck pulling out at the same time. "Maybe they live here." She said noticing the 678 on the plates. But the nagging feeling she got after the truck continued to follow her, let her know that couldn't be further from the truth.

She watched in her rearview mirror as they tried to fall back in traffic as if she was not the intended target. She pulled into the restaurant parking lot, and just as it did before, the truck kept straight.

She kept a small caliber handgun in her glove compartment; she had never had to use it and hoped she would never have to. But until she knew what part of her life had come back to haunt her, she would be prepared.

Toni entered the restaurant and instantly noticed the Deacon. He was seated at a booth by the window with books sprawled across the table. She admired how intelligent he looked as she approached him.

"Good afternoon Deacon James." Toni smiled. He stood to greet her.

"Afternoon sistah." He said while motioning for her to have a seat across the table.

"Thank you for taking time out of your schedule to meet with me." Toni pretended to be meek.

"Well, I'm here for anyone that's struggling with their spirituality. So what did you have questions about specifically?" He asked staying focused.

"Actually, my initial question is about you. You seem so convicted. How do you resist the temptations that I'm sure you experience every day?" Now Toni's chin rested on her fist as she sat attentively waiting for the Deacon's response.

"Well, Ms. Danes." The Deacon began.

"Toni." She corrected him.

"Um, Toni, I don't claim to be perfect. But I do however; pride myself on putting God first. Remembering that everything I endure is God's battle with Satan over my soul. Looking at the bigger picture helps me remember what's important about this life. And that is, the choices I make to determine who my soul ultimately belongs to. We get lost and caught up in everyday life to the point that when the devil is working, we just accept it as if that's the way things are supposed to be.

Before learning about who our Lord and Savior is, we are unaware of the spiritual powers we possess. And resisting temptation is at the top of that list. Once you learn to operate in the Spirit, the material things will start to mean less and less." The Deacon preached.

"What about sex?" Toni interjected as if she hadn't heard a word he said, and trying to make him uncomfortable in the process.

"What about it?" The Deacon asked seriously. Now Toni was uncomfortable.

"I meant, how do you resist it? She tried to pretend they were talking about her issues, but her line of questioning was her way of prying into his life.

"Simple, I'll have sex when God sends me my wife. Until then, I will remain celibate. Plus, I don't put myself in a position to have to resist. The Bible tells us it is better to marry than to burn and frankly Toni, I don't want to burn." The Deacon stated.

"So are you tryna say you're a virgin?" Toni asked with utter confusion.

Deacon James erupted in laughter. "Of course not! I wasn't born a Christian. Believe me, I have had a lot to give up and overcome. It's been a process, it didn't happen overnight." He stared intensely at her, as if to inform her of her future process.

"Well well well, funny meeting you here." Toni and the Deacon were both jolted from their eye contact by the sound of Jojo's voice.

"Wuz up Mah? Who is dis nigga?" Jojo asked sounding as ghetto as he could possibly sound.

"First of all, this is DEACON James, fool!" Toni said rolling her eyes at him. "Deacon, this idiot is Jojo?" She finished her introductions.

"Good afternoon." Deacon James extended his hand even though he was insulted by being called a nigga.

"Yeah whateva." Jojo waved the Deacon off. "Anyway, I need to holla at you Toni. Jo added.

"Then call me." Toni said while giving him an evil eye.

"Don't nobody care about you talking to that square ass nigga, I need to holla at you now!" Jojo raised his voice, getting the attention of the staff and the few patrons in attendance, not to mention the Deacon.

"Please excuse me Deacon James, I apologize for this." She said to the Deacon with a regretful expression that instantly turned to rage the moment she was alone with Jojo. They barely got through the doors of the restaurant before she hit him with a barrage of questions.

"What the fuck are you doing here? Are you following me? What do you want? And must you be a heathen everywhere you go, damn?" She shot them all his way without waiting for a response. She was flaming mad.

Jojo finally spoke. "Peaches know." He told her.

"You told her?" She asked.

"Not quite." He was slightly embarrassed. "Just know she know and she ain't happy."

"Did she tell Rome?" Toni asked with concerned.

"Naw, she won't do that, at least not yet. I'm a try to smooth some shit over. But watch yo back. She might try to run up on you in the mall or something." He chuckled, although Toni saw nothing funny. "In the meantime, answer your fucking phone." Jojo's expression turned back serious. Then he walked away.

Toni observed as he got into a white Lexus. She was confused all over again. She was sure the minute he walked up to the table, that it must've been Jojo driving the blue Mercedes truck. But seeing him in the Lexus had her baffled all over again. She still had so many unanswered questions, and Jojo's surprise appearance didn't help the situation.

Toni was slightly embarrassed to re-enter the restaurant, but she did. She approached the table and sat in silence.

"Is everything alright?" The Deacon asked with genuine concern.

Her expression held so much; anger, confusion, pain, shame. But what he was more concerned about was the hope he saw inside all of that. He didn't want it to get lost in the midst of the confusion in her life.

"It's fine. Everything is fine." She said sounding the opposite of her words.

"Hungry?" Deacon James asked.

She sat up in her seat to shake off the last few minutes and return to a jovial mood.

"Yes, of course Deacon. I could eat." She smiled.

"It's David, call me David." He smiled back.

He could see that there was a lot going on with her, but he wanted to really know who she was so he could help her. In order to do that, he had to get her to let her guard down, even if it meant letting his down too.

Executive Decisions

As Red looked at her savings account balance, she began to regret her decision to stand up Mr. Grant. Although she had to admit that her weekend with Romero was fabulous. Peaches had already informed her of the plan to remove Toni from the equation, after she told her of Jojo and Toni's indiscretions.

Red usually wouldn't get involved in such "foolishness" as she called it. But she could not help but think of how much fun it would be to play with Rome again. She smiled to herself. No one had ever made her feel the way he did. She would have never thought that someone so hardcore could be so sensual and attentive. It was always her showing all the attention, so it was beautiful to have someone cater to her needs for a chance. But now it was time to get back to work. She had to make it up to Mr. Grant and make him believe she was apologetic about her no show.

Getting her finances in order was a priority and she didn't depend on anyone but him. Friends were not important to her because she didn't trust women.

And her sister was the only family she was in contact with on a regular basis. Therefore, she had no time to waste fantasizing.

Red was snapped out of her thoughts by the sound of her cell phone.

"Hello." Red answered.

"So, have you talked to him yet?" The excitement in Peaches' voice was almost annoying to Red.

"Talked to who?" Red asked irritated with the question.

"Romero, duh!" Now Peaches was annoyed.

"Look Peach, I have other business to handle. I can't be pining over a nigga that's all the way in Atlanta!" She couldn't believe that Peaches thought this nonsense would take priority in her life.

"No, you look! I got a plan and people in place. That bitch is gone know what it means to get fucked over." Peaches said with vengeance in her voice. Red rolled her eyes at the phone.

"Girl you doing too much over some dick, that's not yours." Red said trying to bring some reality to the situation.

"Yeah whatever, you just treat Rome like you treat that white man. I need him wrapped around your little finger. And let's not forget, He ain't no broke nigga so it ain't like you would be wasting your time." Peaches reminded her.

"I feel like I'm being pimped. It seems real convenient that you didn't tell me about Toni and Rome's relationship before I went to Atlanta." Red said with suspicion.

"Sistah, can u just make sure you call Romero today and stop over thinking shit. I just found out she was smashing Jojo, damn!" Peaches was trying to convince Red that she didn't already have suspicions about them.

Her anger about this situation even surprised her. She wasn't sure if she was angrier with Toni or Jojo, she just knew her focus was on Toni. She could have told Rome and risked causing and all out war between the friends.

She felt a man was going to be a man and if it's thrown at him, he's going to take it. But when it came to Toni, she felt betrayed. And the jealousy she harbored for her didn't help the situation much.

"I'll see what I can do." Red finally said before hanging up now feeling more involved than before.

She assumed Peaches just wanted to make Toni jealous, but now she felt as if something more sinister was brewing. Even though Toni was not one of her favorite people, she still wasn't sure if she wanted anything to do with it. Then she thought about Romero. "Okay, maybe I'll involve myself a little bit." She said to herself out loud.

After ending her call with Peaches, she decided it was time to pull out the big guns for Mr. Grant. She was against sending pictures over the World Wide Web but she knew she had to get his attention. Red sent the sexiest topless photo she had to Mr. Grant's personal inbox. In minutes, he was texting to set up a date. She responded as usual that she would be there with bells on.

Then she picked up the phone again and dialed a number she had saved in speed dial.

"Hello sexy." A masculine voice said on the other end of the phone.

"Hello yourself." Red said unable to control her smile.

"I'm glad you called and I hope you enjoyed Atlanta as much as it enjoyed you." Romero said talking in code.

"Oh, I enjoyed it alright." She was talking in a code of her own.

"When can I see you again?" Romero asked.

"You say that like I live around the corner. You can always come to the Big Apple, you know?" Red extended an invite.

"I may just take you up on that. Does that invitation include a place to stay?" He questioned.

"Of course! I'm glad to return the favor, all of them if I can. I'll have us a night out on the town planned as well. Just let me know when you'll be in town." She told him.

"Will do, I'll try for next week. I can't make any promises but I will make a way to see you, soon." He wanted her to know he was sincere.

"Alright then, keep me posted. I'm looking forward to your visit. Talk to you later." Red ended the call.

She looked around her apartment. It was nowhere near the size of Romero's home, but it wasn't too shabby either. She lived in the Milan Apartments on East 55th Street. It was more than eighteen hundred square feet with two bedrooms in midtown. The view was beautiful and the apartment was spacious. Her all white and chrome décor brought brightness to the place that unnatural light couldn't touch.

After admiring her decorative decisions, Red began to prepare for her evening with Mr. Grant

The Four Seasons

After retrieving a key from the front desk, Red made her way to the Penthouse Suite. She carried a bag full of goodies for Mr. Grant. She was prepared to show him how apologetic she was. When she entered the room, she noticed there was no gift waiting for her.

"He must be really mad." She thought. So she got to work. Red had three bags of rose pedals that she strategically placed in a trail on the floor, leading to a bubble bath. She changed the hotel sheets to the black satin sheets she bought especially for the occasion.

Noticing the time, Red got dressed in her sexiest Victoria Secrets bra and panty set. She sprawled across the rose pedal covered bed. Just as she began to doze off she heard the suite door open. She played sleep, trying to look as sexy and angelic as possible.

"You whores are all alike." Red heard a female voice say.

Red jumped to her feet pulling the satin sheet with her. She covered her body as she stared at the decrepit old white woman.

"Who in the hell are you? I think you have the wrong room." Red insisted.

"My name is Hilary Grant. I believe you know my late husband, Jonathan Grant." The woman said matter of factly.

"Late?" Red said almost in a whisper.

She realized that had to be the reason she hadn't heard from him. Her knees felt weak and her stomach felt sick. For the first time Red realized she actually cared for Mr. Grant.

"Yes late!" Mrs. Grant yelled with no sympathy or sense of mourning in her tone. "The bastard had a heart attack a week ago. The bottom line is, I could care less about you knowing or how you feel. You are Drea Mason, right? I don't want to get his whores mixed up." Mrs. Grant ranted.

"Right." Red answered reluctantly.

"Well my attorney advised me, against my will, to give you this." She held up a manila envelope and threw it on the bed. "I don't see how women like you live with yourselves." Mrs. Grant scowled before she walked out of the hotel room and slammed the door behind her.

Red sat on the edge of the bed in disbelief of what just transpired. Then she picked up the envelope with an attorney, Rebman and Associates, on the front. She opened the envelope and thumbed through the documents. There was a lot of legal paperwork with her name on it, but the one that caught her attention was the last page, a cashier's check for $750,000.00.

Mr. Grant actually put her in his will, she was in utter disbelief. Although she felt she was well deserving of it, it was a bitter sweet end to their affair. She thought to herself, she would miss Mr. Grant, but thankfully she won't have to miss his money. "Rest in peace Jonathan."

Trust No One

G. Styles, the video producer from LA, contacted Toni about a video shoot in Miami. She had been spending time here and there with David. Although she enjoyed his company and wisdom, it wasn't putting any money in her pocket. She felt enlightened by their conversation and bible study, but she wasn't ready to commit to the lifestyle just yet.

David told the complete truth about his conviction to stay celibate. She had never seen a man with so much self-control, especially around her. He was always sure to keep their meetings in a public place and strictly platonic.

Toni's phone vibrated with a text from Rome. "All is well?" Was all the text read. Toni sent back thumbs up. She still heard from him every day in some form or another, so she figured the news about her and Jojo was still under wraps. She still kept her guard up when it came to Peaches, because she hadn't said anything to Rome but she was sure she hadn't heard all she was going to hear about the situation. But for now she would focus on Miami.

Toni review the information G. Styles gave her over the phone. "Fontainebleu Miami Beach Hotel, Room 1101." She read aloud. She had never been given a specific room number when going to shoot for a video. But she figured for now she would just follow instructions.

Ivey and Toni never seemed to be at the Condo at the same time, so Toni wrote Ivey a note telling her the details of her trip and when she would return. She figured there was far too much going on now to keep her whereabouts a secret.

This time she caught a cab to the airport. Toni thought it best that no one be able to follow her by recognition of her car. The red and black Batman Camaro drew enough attention already.

Toni's cell phone rang as the cab driver put her bags in the trunk.

"Hello." She answered without looking at the caller ID.

"Hey there, you were weighing heavy on my mind and just wanted to check on you. I figured if you were available we could do a lunch study as well." David offered.

"Well actually, I was just on my way to the airport. I have some business in Miami." She told him contemplating whether or not she should just change her plans.

The trip was strictly about the money. It seemed the more time she spent with David, the less desire she had to do the things she usually did. But those desires weren't gone away completely.

"I really hate that I missed you. Well, I pray you a safe trip and a safe return. We'll get together when you get back. God bless sistah." David said with slight disappointment.

"Thank you David, I will definitely let you know when I'm back in town. Talk to you later." She ended her call feeling like a school girl just as the driver closed the trunk. Something about Deacon David James made her feel that way.

"Where to?" The driver asked.

"Lambert Airport."

Four hours later

Toni arrived in Miami after what seemed like the longest two and a half hour flight she had ever been on. She was tired and needed to rest. It was only noon and the video shoot didn't start until 4 pm. She figured that gave her a little time to get rested and freshen up. When she arrived at baggage claim, there was a tall white man dressed in a tuxedo holding a sign with her name on it.

"Impressive." She said to herself. The man she assumed was her driver escorted her to a black, late model, Lincoln Town Car. Within minutes they were pulling up the hotel entrance. Toni tipped the driver before turning to admire how beautiful the hotel was. She tried to contain her excitement as the rich tourist, businessmen, and socialites scurried around as if they were exiting a Motel 6.

She retrieved her key from the front desk as instructed and was escorted to her suite by the bellman. The friendly Hispanic man carried her bags into her suite with a smile on his face the whole time. She tipped him handsomely because she couldn't imagine waiting on someone hand and foot, and remain happy while doing it.

Toni entered the suite and realized just how beautiful it was. The living room held a huge flat screen TV with plush white carpet and white furniture. The refrigerator and mini bar were well stocked and the ice bucket was full.

She opened the curtains to reveal a spacious, private balcony that overlooked the ocean. The king bedroom suite was equally as beautiful with its identical balcony. Toni turned on the shower, got undressed, and began to unpack her bags.

Before entering the bathroom to shower, Toni heard someone enter her room. "Hello! Excuse me but I didn't request housekeeping!" Toni yelled from the other room. Just then, G. Styles entered the doorway of the bedroom. He was not at all attractive. He was dark skinned, with what looked like two sets of teeth. Plus, he looked like he had lifted one too many weights. The sad part was, he thought he was fine with his steroid induced physique.

"Glad to see you getting comfortable." He said trying to sound sexy, but all Toni saw was a lustful lizard.

"Um, can I help you G?" Toni asked trying to figure out how and why he was in her room.

"I'm tryna make sure you ready for dis gig." He said undoing the belt on his pants.

"I'll be ready. I don't need any assistance, thank you." Toni said with a look of disgust on her face as she tried to get a grip on what was really happening.

"Look baby, this is a video with Drake. You play the part of his main chick, you know, the love interest. So you will be the focus of everybody's attention." He told her as he continued to undress. By this point, he was down to his boxers. "So, for an opportunity like that, I figured you'd be willing to offer me some incentive." Now his privates were exposed and he was stroking the ugliest penis she had ever seen.

"Okay, I was tryna be nice, but get yo' black ass out of my room, and put yo' clothes back on!" Toni screamed to the top of her lungs.

G. Styles stomped across the room before she could blink. SMACK! He slapped her so hard she fell into the bathroom and onto the floor.

"Bitch, this is my room and my mutha fucking world! So if you can't get with the program, get yo' ass back on the plane! It's plenty of hoes that'll beg to be in yo' position!" He screamed as he stood over her.

Toni couldn't believe she had been caught off guard like that. She just lay there on the floor of the bathroom holding her face. She watched him intensely, trying to contemplate his next move.

Slowly, she sat up with her back to the bathroom wall. She wanted to be able to at least kick him if he charged her again. Sitting there with anger in her eyes, she tried to hold back angry tears. She didn't want to give him any power by appearing weak. This was one time she wished she could use the gun Romero gave her, she was furious.

"I know you don't think I'm about to take no pussy? It's bitches throwing pussy left and right to be where you sittin'. Baby girl it look like you got a decision to make. But don't take too long, cuz I'll replace yo' ass." G. Styles said as he got dressed to leave. "Oh yeah, and don't ever disrespect me!" He slammed the door.

Toni knew there was nothing to think about. She slept with who she wanted and refused to be bullied by anyone, even for money. Not to mention, he broke her number one rule; No violence, unless she asked for it.

Without a thought, Toni packed her belongings and caught a cab back to the airport. She got an ice pack for her face and bid farewell to Miami.

"It was fun while it lasted. Well not really. I should have gone to lunch."

Undeniable

The more time Red and Romero spent together, the more inseparable they became. In two months' time, Rome visited Red in New York, then she returned to Atlanta with him, and a week later he wouldn't allow himself to stay in Atlanta without her, so he went back to New York for another week.

During his rendezvous with Red, Rome still made sure Toni was safe. Almost against his will, Toni seemed to have become a permanent fixture in his life. Since Red satisfied all of his sexual needs, he and Toni had not seen or had sexual contact with one another in months. However, he still felt the need to watch over her from afar.

Since receiving her newfound riches, Red had no reason to work. But since she and Romero had become somewhat of an item, she wanted to make a business proposal that would legitimize Romero's empire.

She didn't care much for any business that was capable of taking the freedom or life of her or anyone she was involved with. This was the main reason she stayed away from the likes of men like Romero, but their attraction was undeniable. Red had never actually loved a man, so she was having a hard time identifying her feelings.

Rome was equally confused because no matter how much time he spent with Red, Toni was always one of his priorities. In fact, he was not at all confused about his feeling for Toni. He knew he loved her.

But he had a great deal of respect for Red. He loved everything about the way she carried herself. He wondered how a twenty one year old, with a degree in communications, from St. Louis, with no job, lived as well as she did. But he didn't question her; he just enjoyed their time together.

Rome watched Red as she lay on the plush white carpet in front of the fifty one inch flat screen television. She wore nothing but a thong while she laughed at old Martin episodes.

"Whatchu know about this show youngsta? You was minus ten when this was on the air." Romero teased.

"Whatever Grandpa." Red said rolling her eyes at him.

"I ain't Grandpa when you taking all this." He said grabbing his crotch.

"Nope, you daddy." She said playfully putting her foot between his legs. "Have you thought about my offer?" She said changing the subject.

"I'm still thinking about it. But I don't think you understand how hard it is to just leave the game. These niggas out here ain't playin' wit they money, Red. I can't just say "I'm going legit" and niggas gone be like "Aw dats cool homie, good luck", it don't work like that. So even if I do go legit, it's gone take some time." He schooled Red.

She looked at him suspiciously. She wasn't sure if this was a street nigga stalling to stay in the streets or if he was being genuine.

"What?" He asked her wondering why she looked at him the way she did.

"Nothing, but a dynasty waits for no man." Red said before returning to Martin.

"So whatchu saying, you got other investors?" Rome said with a tinge of jealousy.

"Investors? Romero, I don't need any investors. I only asked if you wanted to be involved so you could go legit. Because just fyi, if you get busted, the judge broke us up, flat out." She told him seriously.

"Damn just like that?" He asked.

"I've never given you the impression that your lifestyle is okay with me. As a matter of fact, since the beginning I've been very honest about how I feel." She reminded him of their conversations about his business.

"I feel like you tryna change a nigga." He said.

"I'm just trying to change your outcome baby, that's all." Red stood and walked over to the chair he rested in and kissed his forehead. Her breast dangled in his face and it was impossible for him to resist the urge to grab then suck them both. He did just that as she straddled his lap and released him from his jogging pants. She slowly lowered her wetness onto his massive ten inch shaft. She still had a hard time getting use to how well-endowed he was.

They both sighed with pleasure as he entered her perfectly shaved love box. Rome was turned on by how wet she got and always stayed. She rode him slowly at first as he sucked and massaged her breast. Red leaned back to allow the head of his penis to stroke her g spot. Her body began to convulse right before she released a flood of juices into his lap. He almost screamed when his nut erupted while Red vigorously rode him until her orgasm was complete.

"Damn you got some good pussy!" Romero roared.

"Good enough to go legit?" Red said with a sexy smile as she took one of her breast in her hand and licked her nipple.

His penis instantly began to pulsate. He rested it against her clit and began to slowly roll his hips.

"Now tell me about this business." He said with his voice sounding deep and sexy.

"It's an en-ter-tain-ment comp-an-y. But I need you to run the main-ten-ance com-pa-ny from At-lan-ta." Red was barely able to speak while Rome worked her clit over with the head of his dick.

"Okay we'll discuss the details after you suck all yo nut off this dick." He was testing her level of freakiness.

Before he could finish his statement, she stood up, dropped to her knees and took all of him into her mouth. Rome grabbed her hair as he threw his head back in pleasure.

"Damn! You win! Consider that our handshake. Shit!

Surprise Visit

Ivey and Toni's mother, Lois, was sure to make financial provisions for her girls. At age twenty one, they were both given entitlement to the payout on the life insurance policy Lois had in place for them. Both women cashed out on their $350,000.00 cash benefits.

Ivey paid off her student loans and had begun to plan her wedding. She and Brandon had plans to start a non-profit organization and buy their first home together as well.

Toni, on the other hand, put her money in the bank and let Romero and the videos take care of her. But since the incident with G. Styles, she had pushed pause on the video work.

Spending time with David was satisfying on an intellectual and spiritual level, but physically she was starved and she missed Romero. She hadn't been touched by a man since G. Styles slapped her off her feet, so she decided to pay Romero a surprise visit because she knew she was always welcomed in his home.

It was the beginning of spring and the weather in Atlanta was beautiful. The temperature was in the eighties, a tad warmer than in St. Louis. She got a rental car from the airport and headed to Romero's.

Just as Toni pulled into the circular driveway at Romero's, her phone rang, it was Rome. She was shocked that he called, because they usually communicated via text message unless there was something of importance to discuss. She figured she was already there, so she didn't answer.

Toni retrieved her bags from the backseat and headed to the side door. Romero had given her keys to that entrance in case she was in town and he wasn't. He always wanted her to have a place to stay.

She rustled with her keys to find the key to the door. Just as she was about to stick her key in the lock, Rome snatched the door open, stepped outside, and closed the door behind him.

"Hey baby! Whatchu doin' here? It's not really a good time." Romero told Toni nervously.

"Romero, there had better be a shark chasing a pit-bull behind this door or you better let me in if you don't want these nice neighbors to call the police." Toni threatened. Of course the police were the last people Romero wanted to see, but he feared if he let her in, their presence would be inevitable.

The problem was, when Rome returned to Atlanta, Red came back with him. It wasn't planned at all, but neither was Toni's visit. Before Rome could say another word, Toni pushed past him and into the house. She made a beeline for Rome's bedroom to find out what or who he was hiding. Rome was hot on her heals trying to catch her, but he was too late. Toni opened the door to a naked Red sprawled across Rome's king sized bed. Toni saw Red, literally.

"What the fu....?" Toni couldn't even finish her sentence.

Red jumped out of bed and grabbed the sheet to cover her body.

"What is she doing here?" Red asked pointing in Toni's direction.

"Naw, Bitch what the fuck are you doing here? You invading my territory, but something tells me you knew that already." Toni said thinking of Peaches payback.

"I've been up and through here for over a month. This territory seems to be unclaimed if you ask me." Red responded with an attitude.

They stood face to face again. Only this time they weren't children and this was not about Ivey.

Toni charged, punching Red square in the face. She caught her off guard which caused Red to stumble. Red quickly recovered in retaliation. The two women fought with the anger of rabid dogs. Rome tried to get between them but was met with a barrage of flying fists.

Jojo heard the commotion from downstairs and rushed upstairs to find out what was going on. He entered Rome's room to find him caught in the middle of the brawl between Red and Toni. Red was naked all over again and Toni wasn't far behind. Her blouse had been ripped almost completely off, so all she wore was a pair of denim booty shorts. Jo helped Rome break up the fight before they did permanent damage to his house and themselves.

Jo grabbed Toni by the waist and carried her into his bedroom. She was still trying to get to Red.

"Calm yo ass down girl!" Jojo yelled trying to get her to stop struggling.

"You knew he was fucking with her? You could've told me something, you tell me everything else. Got me out in this mutha fucka looking stupid and shit! Toni screamed with hurt and anger in her voice. "How in the fuck did they....you know what, never mind. I already know Peaches is behind this shit!" Toni said as she made her way down to the side door, where her bags still lay outside the door.

"Where are you going?" Jojo asked her.

"Back the fuck to St. Louis! Fuck Atlanta! Fuck Rome! Fuck Red!

Fuck Peaches! And Fuck you! Toni screamed before slamming the door.

Before pulling away Toni sat in the driver's seat with her head on the steering wheel. She shed a few tears then looked at herself in the mirror. The face looking back at her was unrecognizable. Her mascara was running and there was blood and scratches all over her face. Fresh bruising had even started to appear.

Toni's vanity would not allow her to go through the airport or return to St. Louis looking the way she did. She decided to stay in Atlanta long enough to nurse her wounds. She booked a room at the Sheraton in Downtown Atlanta. Toni threw on a pair of Tom Ford shades hoping they would hide enough of her face so the bruising wouldn't be noticeable.

Getting undressed was the first thing she did once she arrived to her suite. Toni stood in the full length mirror and looked at the damage done by Red, wondering what Red looked like. Her right eye was staring to swell along with the cut on her mouth. "That little bitch fucked me up." Toni admitted while applying the ice pack to her face.

All she could think about was how every time she turned David down to meet for study, something bad happened. "I shoulda kept my ass at home." She said to herself as she slipped into the bubble bath she had run immediately after she entered her room.

Toni soaked until the water was almost cold. She finally got out of the tub after almost an hour and slipped into her robe.

Knock Knock Knock! She was momentarily startled because she wasn't expecting anyone.

"Who is it?" Toni asked through the door.

"Ma'am, you left your ID at the front desk." A male voice said from the hallway.

She was sure she remembered putting her ID in her wallet but without looking, she opened the door anyway.

"I think you have the wro…." She stopped talking at the sight of Romero standing in the hallway.

She immediately tried to close the door, but he moved faster. Rome blocked her from closing the door and forced his way in. She gave up once she realized it was no use fighting, plus she was tired of fighting at this point. There was no point in asking how he knew where she was because he had people everywhere, so it was just a matter of time before he knew she was still in Atlanta.

"Whatchu want?" She asked as she walked away from him, leaving him standing at the door.

"I want to apologize to you. We always been honest with each other and I know I shouldnt've fucked with her. I'm being honest now and I don't know what it is about her but I couldn't resist, I tried. This might not even be the right time for this Toni but, I love you. I've been in love with you for a long time. But a nigga can't tell you nothing like that without you looking at me sideways. So, I accept our relationship as it is, so I can keep you in my life. But now, you need to make a decision. I'm a grown ass man Toni. You can't just keep a mufucka in limbo.

Now it's yo call. I admit, I like her, but if you decide to really be in my life, I'll let her go. No matter what you decide I'll be here for you. But if not, you gotta let me go man. Let me be with who I wanna be with." He told her still standing at the door, but he held her attention like they were standing face to face.

Toni was still stuck on "I love you". She cared about him but love was something Toni couldn't quite grasp. She felt it was just another way to make a person weak in order to control them. She cared more about Romero than she had any man, so losing him would not only be hard, but it would hurt.

Toni stood, disrobed, and walked up to Romero. She looked up at him with teary eyes, and then she slapped him. He didn't move or protest, in fact, he felt he deserved it for hurting her. Then she grabbed his face and kissed him more passionately than he could ever remember coming from her.

He picked her up and she wrapped her legs around his waist. He walked to the bed and gently lay Toni down while still kissing her. Toni made love to Romero for the first time that night. And with all the explosive sexual encounters they've shared, He couldn't deny that this one would be unforgettable.

Rome awoke the next morning to Toni watching him.

"Good morning babe." He said with his tone groggy.

"Good morning. So where's Red?" Toni interrogated catching him completely off guard.

"She flew back to New York. She was a little embarrassed about how she looked." He said. Toni tried to hide the fact that she was proud of herself.

"Is she coming back?" Toni asked

"That's up to you." Rome said

"I can't give you want you want Romero. You deserve to be with somebody that can love you back. I'm in the middle of trying to figure out how to love myself. I care enough about you to let you go. But don't you let that bitch make you cut me off." They both laughed at Toni's comment.

"Neva dat baby. I always got you." He gave her one last kiss before he got dressed to leave.

As he left, he realized Toni had already put her copy of his house key in his pants pocket. He looked at the key and shook his head at the thought of what could have been.

Toni sat in her suite, still steaming mad about her situation, but relieved that Rome still didn't know about her and Jojo. She would have to accept the situation and move on. All she knew is that it will be extremely difficult to replace Romero Wallace.

Rock Bottom

After a week of being high on Percocet, cush, and 1800 silver tequila, Toni managed to get her appearance almost close to normal. She hadn't heard from Romero that entire time and she had to admit to herself that she already missed his daily check ups on her. She agreed to let him go, so she resisted the urge to contact him as well.

Her wounds were healed and she was ready to get home to St. Louis. So she packed her bags and caught the next flight home. Still in a drug and alcohol induced haze, Toni slept the entire flight and cab ride back to Ivey's.

When she arrived Toni took her bags to the guestroom and undressed for a shower. Figuring since no one else was there, she would take the liberty of walking around nude. She missed being able to do so at her house, so she used this small amount of alone time to be in the buff.

Toni put her Pandora on the Maxwell station and showered long enough to use up all the hot water in the complex. She still felt loopy from her last few days of intoxication, but the shower seemed to assist in her sobriety just a little bit. When she exited the bathroom still naked, she came face to face with Brandon.

With no boundaries or shame, Toni stood inside the doorway with a sexy smirk on her face. She never attempted to cover her naked body.

"See something you like?" She asked Brandon with seduction in her voice.

"Toni, would you put some clothes on please?" Brandon asked with insistence.

"I will if you stop looking at my titties." She was actually amused by their interaction in her half high state of mind.

"Toni to be honest, I don't care how attractive you are, you're one of the ugliest people I know, so believe me you have nothing I want to look at. And if you can't respect yourself at least respect your sister, and put some clothes on!" This time his voice was elevated.

"And when you're done, pack your things and get out of my house!" Ivey said from behind Brandon. Neither of them was aware that she had been standing in the doorway from the moment she heard Toni's voice. "No matter how much I do for you or how many times I forgive you for dogging me, you continue to treat me like I mean nothing to you.

I've tried to just accept you for who you are and love you anyway. Well I love you sistah, but I cannot continue to accept you treating me like you do every other woman on the street. I've done nothing but be there for you now I'm done. You don't care about anyone but yourself, so that's where you should be, by yourself. Please be gone when I get back." The calm in Ivey's voice was more frightening than if she had screamed to the top of her lungs.

She was at her wit's end with Toni and now with her advance toward her soon to be husband, she had enough. As Ivey left the condo she thought about how hard it would be, but she would have to love her sister from afar.

Five years ago

At age sixteen Ivey was beginning to recognize her interest in the opposite sex. The main reason was Dante Hill, he was a year older but they shared several classes in school. She and Toni attended McClure High School; Ivey was at the end of her sophomore year and Toni was about to graduate.

Dante was a junior and was wanted by half the females in the school. Part of his popularity was because of his spot on the varsity basketball team, but mainly because of how attractive he was. He was six foot three with a golden complexion. He kept his naturally curly hair cut low and it didn't help that his eyes were the same color as his skin.

Dante first noticed Ivey in their current events class during a discussion about social acceptance and peer pressure. Usually she sat quiet and did her work but her passion about this topic made her put herself in the spotlight, and Dante noticed her. He hadn't even notice how pretty she was before, but once he did, he would never forget. He hung on to her every word and at the end of class he had to talk to her.

"Excuse me, Ivey?" Dante tapped her shoulder to get her attention.

"Yes?" Ivey was sure this conversation was about tutoring or something else impersonal.

"Hi, I'm Dante." He said extending his hand.

She shook his hand but still waited for him to get to his point.

"I know who you are, but how can I help you?" She stated giving him her undivided attention.

"I was wondering if I could call you some time." He said slightly nervous.

Ivey was caught off guard and it was obvious from her actions. She fumbled around with her book and papers then finally responded.

"Um, well, I guess. I mean, yes of course you can." She started to write her number on a piece of paper.

"Here, use this." Dante handed her his cell phone.

She took the phone and saved her number in his contacts. As she handed him the phone, she looked at him seemingly for the first time, and noticed how attractive he was.

"I'll be in touch." He told her interrupting her gaze.

"Okay." Ivey gave a shy smile and headed to her next class.

When they talked, everything fit like a puzzle. They dated the entire summer and Ivey would have considered him her first love.

School was about to start, so Dante spent as much time with Ivey as he could before the summer ended. Lois had fallen ill, so they spent most of their time at Ivey's. They saw the occasional movie, but Ivey needed to be close to her mother and Dante understood.

Toni had graduated and spent most of her time running the streets and running away from their mother's sickness.

Lately, Dante had started to pressure Ivey about sex and they even argued about it on several occasions. But their worst argument would be their last.

"I told you, I'm not having sex until I get married! It's not up for discussion. You thought I was lying when I told you that in the beginning?" Ivey said completely frustrated that they were having this conversation again.

"I'm just sayin', we gone be together forever, right? So what difference does it make?" He said just as frustrated, in more ways than one. "This is some bullshit! You know how many girls throwin' it at me!" He felt the need to remind her.

They sat next to one another on the couch, but his comment made Ivey feel the need to get away from him. She stood and walked to the other side of the room.

"First of all, don't you ever talk to me like that! And secondly, I don't care how many girls are throwing it at you. If they don't care about their virtue, that's on them because you clearly don't. But if you're gonna sleep with 'em, do it and leave me alone. Otherwise don't you EVER throw another woman in my face again!" Ivey had to get some air; she stormed out of the house and slammed the screen door.

Dante sat looking as dumb as he felt when Toni entered the room. She heard the entire argument along with several others on the same topic. Toni wore a white tank top with the shortest pair of denim shorts she owned.

"I told you she ain't uppin that precious lil pussy of hers. But I can introduce you to some grown woman shit." Toni said seductively.

"Aw yeah?" Dante said as his eyes went from her lips down to her thick milk chocolate thighs.

"What about Ivey?" He asked still focused on her voluptuous body.

"What she don't know won't hurt her." Toni said *walking close to Dante and then putting her bare foot between his legs to caress his erection. At age eighteen she was already a seductress. Just as his eyes closed and his head fell back, Ivey entered the house.*

"Wow, so I guess my sister is at the top of that list." Ivey *was completely disgusted with them both.* *"GET OUT, IT'S OVER!"* Ivey *screamed pointing him in the direction of outside.*

Dante was too ashamed to protest, he just left without a word. Ivey stared at Toni and waited for her to say anything. But all she got was a nonchalant empty stare back at her.

Ivey couldn't believe she shared the same blood with a person so self involved that she didn't even care how her actions affected the people she was supposed to love. But she did and there she was, Antoinette Alexis Danes in all her egotistical glory.

Ivey knew expressing her distain to Toni would mean nothing, so she left her standing in the living room, alone, exactly how she would end up if she didn't change her ways in Ivey's opinion.

Present day

For the first time in her life, Toni actually felt remorseful because of her actions. The more sober she became the

134

more she realized the magnitude of what she had done to Ivey.

A flood of emotions came over her as she packed her belongings. She cried out loud for the first time in years. Toni felt as though she was sabotaging everything in her life. First Rome, now the closest person to her had dismissed her from their lives.

She felt defeated and was a slave to her poorly thought out actions. "What the fuck was I thinking? She scolded herself.

She picked up the phone and called the only other person she felt wouldn't pass judgment on her, Deacon David James. She tried to get her composure as she waited for him to answer the phone.

"Hello sistah, how are you?" David sounded more than happy to hear from Toni.

"Not good, I need to talk, and not in public. I've got a lot going on." Toni told David in a tone that let him know she was serious. He gave her his home address so she could have the privacy she felt she needed. Toni put the address into the GPS on her phone.

"Give me about an hour; I'm in the middle of something." Toni told David still packing her bags.

"Okay, I'll be here." David assured her and still very concerned about what could be going on with her.

"And David?"

"Yes Toni?

"Will you please make me some coffee?" She asked needing to sober up.

"It's already brewing." David told Toni as he got up from his couch to head to the kitchen.

They ended their call, but David couldn't help but be concerned about what he had just done. He prayed this wasn't Satan trying to temp him. From their conversations he could tell there was a lot that came along with Toni, he just hoped that she was coming there strictly for his friendship and support. David prayed for strength while he prepared a pot of coffee and got ready for Toni's visit.

When the doorbell rang David was deep in scripture, brushing up on his lessons about temptation. He opened the door and what he saw broke his heart. Toni stood there with running mascara and dried tears mixed with wet ones. He simultaneously opened the door to let her in while handing her a hot cup of coffee.

"Are you okay?" David asked Toni while escorting her to sit on the couch in his living room. As distraught as she was, Toni still noticed how impressive his house looked with its contemporary décor.

"Nice house." She managed to say through sniffles and sips of coffee.

"Thank you Toni, but are you okay?" He asked her again.

Toni had always had a way of using displacement to avoid handling difficult situations.

"No David, I'm not okay. I'm fucked up. Excuse my language." Toni put her head down. "I'm surprised you trusted me to come here, I wouldn't have." She shed a tear at the thought of how true her statement was. "I don't deserve a friend like you. I'm not a good friend, David. I'm never available when you call, but every time I call you, you're there." Toni opened up to David as he sat across from her holding her hands.

"Toni I'm just a vessel. God is the one that's always there for you. I'm just fortunate enough that he sees fit to use me." He tried to make her understand that her trust and faith in man had been misplaced.

"You don't know me David; I'm not a good person. I've done things that I would be ashamed to tell the devil. It's so much, I can't remember all the things I've done or the people I've hurt." Toni bared her soul to David that day.

She told him everything she could remember about her deceit and betrayal. She also mentioned how she was being followed and getting strange hang up phone calls. He listened to her, held her when she cried, they laughed and they prayed. David rode with Toni on her emotional roller coaster that day, well into the night. He insisted that she spend the night and set her up in his guest room.

It even surprised Toni that she didn't attempt any seduction on her visit with David. But she figured, enough damage had already been done and she didn't want to taint the only pure relationship she had left.

As she drifted off to sleep, she played the scripture over in her head that David read to her:

Jeremiah 29:11
"For I know the plans I have for you," declares the Lord. "Plans to prosper you and not to harm you, plans to give you hope and a future."

Toni slept peacefully for the first time in what seemed like years. Her soul felt cleansed after being able to be true with herself and admit who she really was. Now she needed to figure out who she wanted to be from this day forward.

Aftermath

The smell of breakfast jolted Toni from her peaceful sleep. She forgot where she was for just a few seconds before she got out of bed. She changed into the jogging pants and tee shirt David gave her the night before. They were huge on her. The tee shirt hung past her knees so she decided not to even bother with the pants that seemed ten feet long.

Toni made her way to the kitchen. She walked through the living room and noticed how bright it looked as the sun beamed through the sheer curtains on the large picture window. The house had a warm feel to it. It was more than just a house it felt like a home. She admired the Better Homes and Garden décor as she followed the sound and smell of breakfast into the kitchen.

David was cooking fried potatoes, French toast, turkey bacon, grits, and omelets made to order.

"Good morning sleepy head, you're just in time. What would you like in your omelet? He asked her with a smile bright as the sun.

"Well let's see." She studied the already organized ingredients on the table. "I would like tomatoes, onions, peppers, spinach, mushrooms, jalapenos, and cheddar cheese." She finished placing her order.

"Your order is coming right up." David pretended to be a short order cook. They both laughed.

"How did you sleep?" He asked while preparing her food.

"Very well actually, I can't remember the last time I woke up and felt so rested and peaceful. I don't know if I've ever woke up that way to be honest." She actually took time to try to remember. "Anyway." She snapped out of her thoughts. "How did you sleep?"

"I was able to rest easy knowing I didn't have to worry about you." He admitted.

"Little old me?" Toni joked.

"Yes Toni, I worry about you. And apparently for good reason, judging by the things you've told me." He said referring to last night's confessional.

"I'm a work in progress David." She was being facetious and serious at the same time.

"We all are, trust me." David said as he placed her omelet on the plate in front of her.

The aroma hit her in the face and her stomach began to growl. Toni finished making her plate with the other fixings and headed directly to the kitchen table to eat. She bowed her head and said grace.

"This looks fabulous. Who taught you how to cook like this?" She asked as she dug her fork into the first bite of her omelet. "Mmmmmm!" She continued before he could answer.

"My aunt Joyce raised me. I came to live with her shortly after my parents died in a car accident when I was about six. She taught me how to cook just about anything." He talked as he cooked.

"Oh, where is she?" Toni asked as she looked around for evidence of his aunt.

"She died almost a year ago, cancer. She left the house to me. Her husband is out here somewhere. I assumed they were estranged, but I found out later that he was on drugs, so she left all her affairs to me once she started to get sick." His tone became sad as he spoke of his aunt.

"I'm so sorry." Toni empathized. "Was she your mother or father's sister, if you don't mind me asking?

"My father's, my mom was actually an only child." David continued to reveal.

"All this time I never knew that about you. Am I so needy that all we discuss are my issues? Toni said just now realizing the surface of her selfishness.

"That's okay Toni, that's what I'm ordained to do." He said in a pastoral tone.

"So I'm just a mission for you?" Toni was almost offended.

"Honestly yes, you were somewhat of a mission at first. But I consider you a friend at this point," He told her.

David was having a difficult time keeping his actions in check. It took everything in him, even the silent prayer he said in his head, to not act on the attraction he felt for Toni. She was somewhat of a project when this all began, but now he had begun to see the potential for her. Not to mention her undeniable beauty.

"I'm glad to hear that. A friend is what I need right now." She said as she finished her meal. She sat back in her chair and rubbed her stomach that was full to capacity.

"That meal was wonderful, by the way, thank you. And thank you for your hospitality and your ear. I appreciate it. To be honest, I don't really know what I would've done if you hadn't been there for me last night. I mean you and God." She chuckled a little.

"Anytime, I enjoyed your company. You're actually the first woman to spend the night in this house since my aunt passed. Consider yourself privileged." He winked at her as he removed her plate from the table.

Toni stood up and pushed him to the side playfully.

"Move it busta. You cook, I clean." She snatched the dish towel from his hands and began to wash the breakfast dishes.

Toni was proud of herself for her behavior with David. And even though her attraction to him was irrefutable, she didn't want to taint their newfound relationship.

"When I'm done I'll be heading out, I guess I'll get settled back into my apartment since my sister is done with me." She said clearly disappointed in herself.

"Well, I plan to speak with them; don't worry about that right now. Get settled in and keep me posted." David told her as he left the kitchen. He was headed to church to conduct prayer meeting. "Plus, make sure you lock up when you leave and call me later. Oh, and I expect to see you on Sunday." He said as he back stepped in to the kitchen.

Toni showered and dressed after she finished the dishes, and then drove to her loft. As she drove, she pondered over the day before with David. She couldn't believe she had revealed so much of herself to him. She had never been so vulnerable with anyone before. Even though she felt like an open book, it was refreshing to get to know her for a change. Getting to know David wasn't so bad either, she thought while pulling into the parking garage at her apartment building.

It wasn't hard to find a parking space on a Tuesday mid-morning. She backed into the closest available space to the door, so she could unload her belongings from her car. Toni retrieved the pistol from her glove compartment and continued on to her trunk.

She popped the trunk and began to take the bags, totes, and boxes out of her car. Toni stood after putting the first bag on the ground and noticed the blue Mercedes truck creeping up from the left; she felt a presence behind her. The gun was in her purse and trying to retrieve it would be too obvious. Before she could think of what her next move should be, Toni suddenly felt a sharp pain in the back of her head. Everything went black.

Forgiven Not Forgotten

It had been a few days since Ivey made Toni leave her apartment. Although she was upset, it relieved her to know that the Deacon had seen Toni after their confrontation. He told her that Toni was extremely remorseful and apologetic, so it was perplexing to Ivey why she hadn't heard from her. She had already forgiven her sister, she just knew she would never forget.

Ivey couldn't understand the motivation for most of Toni's actions, but there had to be some underlying reason. She wanted to at least try to scratch the surface of Toni's issues. Her destructive behavior had driven a wedge between them for so long, that Ivey was starting to forget that neither Toni's behavior nor their relationship was typical.

Dealing with the dysfunctional relationship even made it difficult for Ivey to begin her wedding plans. Until now, she wasn't even sure if including her in the wedding party was even possible.

The wedding was three months away and her sister was still considered an alternate bridesmaid. Toni hadn't shown much interest in the wedding or her position in it, so Ivey figured she wouldn't care one way or the other.

Now Brandon on the other hand, wanted Toni as far away from the pulpit as possible. But, he knew how his fiancé felt about her sister being involved, and her feelings were most important to him.

Ivey sat at her desk in her office / guestroom. She went through new and old organizers trying to make sure she didn't leave anyone off the guest list. As she approached the "M" section she saw two names she completely forgot about, Deanna and Drea Mason. She still had both Peaches and Red's contact information. They lost contact and went their separate ways in life but they were still childhood friend and she wanted them to share this special day with her.

She was totally oblivious to the drama brewing between Toni and the two sisters, therefore, she had no reason to deny them invitations to her wedding. She also looked at the invite to her dad and Regina while silently praying for no drama.

"Hey babe." Brandon said as he walked up behind Ivey and kissed her forehead while she looked up at him.

"Hi baby, I'm just getting these invitations together." Ivey sighed.

Brandon looked around the desk and his eyes focused on one envelope in particular. "Is this an invitation for your dad?" Brandon asked her with confusion in his face. Ivey looked up with equally matched confusion.

"Yeah, why?" she asked.

"Because, he should be part of the wedding, that's why. He should be the one to give you away Ivey." He told her as if to explain the wedding procedure to her.

Brandon knew that her relationship with her father was distant, but he didn't realize she never even considered asking him to give her away at her own wedding.

"I was actually going to ask your dad." She admitted.

"Why?" He couldn't understand.

"Because," She sounded exasperated. "My dad's presence does something to Toni." Ivey told Brandon not even realizing how much she had allowed Toni's influence to affect her decisions.

"Baby, do you hear yourself? This isn't Toni's wedding. How can you let her feelings for your father allow you to deny him the opportunity to walk his daughter down the aisle on her wedding day?" Brandon had turned Ivey's chair to face him. He needed her to know how serious he was about this situation.

Ivey realized he was absolutely right. As she thought back in that short moment, she realized that most of the decisions she made regarding their father specifically, was influenced by the way Toni felt about him.

"You're right, and I won't. I'll set up a day so I can ask him officially." She smiled at Brandon with loving eyes. "I love you so much, you know that?" She couldn't believe she had been blessed with a man so wonderful.

"I know I love you more." He smiled back as he bent down to kiss Ivey on the lips.

He grabbed her around the waist and lifted her from the chair. He kissed her passionately. Ivey wrapped her arms around Brandon's neck and reciprocated the gesture.

Ivey was a virgin, but she was no stranger to what she was feeling. Brandon promised that he wouldn't take her before they were married, but it was becoming harder to resist her. It didn't help that she was becoming more and more sexually charged every time they touched.

"Wait, stop." Brandon said into Ivey's mouth as he tried to discontinue the wrestling match their tongues were having.

Ivey reacted as if she heard nothing as she grabbed the back of his head to pull him closer. Brandon had to put an end to this before his manhood took over. He pulled her arms from around his neck in an attempt to slow things down.

"I want you." Ivey said for the first time in her life. That made it so much harder to tell her no.

"Baby we gotta stop. I told you, we're gonna do this right." Brandon tried to say through Ivey's kisses.

She wanted to agree but the closer it came to their wedding day, the harder it was for her to resist him. And the more sexual she became, the harder it was for him to resist what she was trying to give.

"Babe please!" Brandon had actually began to plead with her.

She kissed him one last time. "Okay Okay I'll stop." She said backing away just a little. Brandon adjusted himself to a more comfortable position in his pants and looked up at an extremely sensual Ivey.

"Babe we gotta do premarital counseling. I think it'll help us to stay focused." He said.

"You wanna see a psychiatrist?" She asked.

"Absolutely not, I mean a Pastor."

"I'm not talking to your father about how much I wanna give you some!" She said with a look that said "ew" on her face.

"Me either, that's not cool. I'll ask Deacon James if he can make some time to counsel us." Brandon said liking his own idea.

"That's better. Uugh!" She shuttered again at the thought of discussing sex with Pastor Cameron. "So does this mean I can't touch you until our wedding day?" She asked playfully.

"No, it just means you have to stop trying to seduce me lady." Brandon said snatching Ivey up and kissing her forehead. "I love you." He said.

"I love you more, Mr. Cameron."

Timing is Everything

While pacing back and forth in the bathroom at Romero's, Red frantically called Peaches' cell phone. When she heard the voicemail again, she hung up in frustration. She slammed her phone on the sink so hard, the screen almost cracked. Red stood over the sink looking down at the pregnancy test thinking this was the longest five minutes of her life.

She had never had a pregnancy scare in her life because she was always careful. But with Rome, there were no boundaries. They made love whenever, wherever, and however. It was always completely spontaneous. Now here she was wondering if she was about to be a mother.

When this all began, it was just part of a plot to help Peaches with her revenge, whatever that was, in addition to some enjoyment for herself. She never would have imagined having the feelings she had for Rome, not to mention possibly having his child.

She got butterflies in her stomach that caused her to have to sit down on the edge of the Jacuzzi tub. Red thought back to Romero's behavior over the last week. A few days before, he seemed to become distant. She asked if it was her and if he was okay, but she got the same, "I'm aight" as an answer every time. She had spent enough time around him to know when something wasn't right with him. "Maybe it's business." She said trying to dismiss that fact that Rome could possibly have an issue with her.

They co-existed harmoniously with one another. Romero was slowly legitimizing his business and their sex life was awesome. So Red had no clue as to what could have been bothering him.

The alarm on Red's phone indicating that the test should be ready sounded, jolting her from her thoughts of Romero. She picked up the E.P.T test and stared at the blue plus sign in the result window of the test. "Damn!" was all she could say.

Romero sat in his den staring at his IPhone. He had text Toni several times this week, but she never responded. He knew they agreed to go their separate ways, but he was having a hard time believing that Toni would ignore him. "Don't you let that bitch make you cut me off." Kept playing over in his head. So he knew she intended to stay in touch with him in some way. Not to mention the fact that Toni knew Rome would murder the city if he thought she wasn't safe, so she would be sure to let him know she was alright.

Red stood in the doorway watching Rome as his eyes penetrated the screen on his phone. She noticed he had done that a lot lately. She even tried to unlock his code to find out what was so important to him.

"Hey you." Red said to Rome.

"What's up?" He said not even looking in her direction.

"Are we okay Romero? I mean if it's too much for you to have me around, I do have my own place. I'll go home if you want me to." She said deciding if he gave the wrong answer that he would never know about the baby.

Romero looked her in the eyes and could see the pain she felt from his neglect over the last week. He didn't realize how his preoccupation with Toni was affecting her until now.

He motioned for her to sit on his lap. She approached him while trying not to shed a tear. She was pregnant and emotional. But she did all she could to keep it together.

Before he spoke, he pulled her face to his and kissed her lips. "I'm sorry." He whispered. "I'm happy you here. I got a lot going on but I didn't mean to make you feel like that though. Look, I need to leave town for a few days, and when I get back it's gone be me and you. And you will have my undivided attention." He said kissing her again.

"Where are you going?" She asked taking a step back putting her hands on her hips.

"I got some business to handle baby, but you're welcome to stay here til I get back. Just don't be rambling through my shit." Rome joked seriously. He picked up his phone and began booking his flight.

"We need to talk." Red said very seriously. Rome had already started to get his things together for his trip as Red replaced him in his chair.

"About what?" Rome asked still preoccupied.

"Us." Red beat around the bush.

"I tell you what, when I get back we gone have a romantic evening and we can talk as much about us as you want to. Is that cool?"

"That's cool." Red was nervous enough about telling him about the baby right now. So this gave her an out for the time being.

They said their goodbyes and Rome got in his Range Rover. As he headed to the airport he called Jojo.

"Wuz up my dude?" Jo answered.

"I need you in the Lou ASAP." Rome said.

"Wuz the deal?" Jo questioned.

"I don't know, but something ain't right with Toni, so I'm headed there now." Rome said looking at his cell phone again.

"Aight man, I'm a see what I can do." Jojo casually said.

"Nigga! This is not a request!" Romero commanded.

"Aight nigga damn, I'm there." Jojo figured this was not the time for a back and forth with Romero. Jojo hung up the phone and immediately booked his flight. After that, he tried to call Peaches to see if she had any idea of what Romero was talking about. He got her voicemail. "Please don't have shit to do with this Peach." He said out loud.

There was no way he could let Rome find out about him and Toni like this.

Revenge is a Dish….

Everything was hazy, the light, the sound, her memory. All she could do was try to focus and figure out where she was and what was going on. Toni didn't know how long she had been unconscious, but it felt like weeks.

Her body was numb, but she could tell she was lying down. As she focused her eyes, she could see that her hands were bound to the post of a rusted wrought iron bed. Then she tried to move and realized her feet were bound as well. Toni wanted to scream but thought it better to review her surroundings before alerting anyone that she was awake.

The problem was, she had no idea why she was there. She didn't know who had taken her or where she was. The room was dark and dim, and smelled like a port o potty.

The more coherent she became, the feeling in her body began to return. It was then that she realized how much pain she was in. As much as she could, she lifted her head to observe her naked body. There were bruises everywhere. The more she looked, the more she felt.

"You ready for some more Bitch?" Toni heard a male voice say from the doorway of what appeared to be an abandoned building.

"Wha…" Toni tried to talk but realized her lips were swollen almost shut. This realization triggered the taste of blood in her mouth and the smell of musty nuts and piss in the air.

A large fowl smelling man approached the bed as he unbuckled his pants to unleash his penis. Toni struggled to move but realized there was nothing she could do. He climbed on top of her and penetrated her without a condom. Tears instantly began to stream down her cheeks. He humped and grunted until he finally released himself on Toni's face.

"Ahhhh, yeah bitch, you got some good pussy, you know that?" The man said while still ejaculating in her face.

There was a time when that statement would have been music to her ears, but now she realized how demeaning it was, even in the past.

"Please stop." Is all she managed to get out. Her body felt heavy and she couldn't fight if she wanted to.

"We just getting started baby girl." The vulgar man said as he called five other men into the room to join the party. All six men took turns violating her in ways she had never imagined.

They penetrated her vaginally, orally, anally, and emotionally. Each man as they ejaculated, released it into her face. And anytime she tried to show an ounce of resistance, she was met with painful blows to the face and ribs. She endured this for hours until her body finally gave in and she passed out.

She had never been so violated in her entire life. As she drifted in and out of consciousness, fantasies of being somewhere else drifted in and out of her mind. As she drifted, she recalled her conversations with David, wondering if her prayers would be heard. She felt like what was happening to her was deserved somehow. But she still couldn't help but think that what David told her couldn't be a lie, and God was here for her as well.

"So, we meet again. I bet you didn't think it would be like this, huh?" Toni tried to focus her eyes in the direction the voice was coming from. Just then, Coco immerged from the shadows of the room. She had observed every second of the vulgarities performed on Toni.

"Why?" Toni managed to barely get out in a whisper.

"Are you serious? Don't play dumb with me Bitch!" Coco screamed. She had been waiting for this moment to see Toni suffer.

All Toni could do was shake her head "no" in protest. She honestly didn't understand what was happening to her or why.

"Well since you a dumb slut, let me refresh your memory."

Bottoms Up

Saturday night always promised to be a packed night at Bottoms Up Strip Club. Toni and Coco made their way through the crowd to the stripper's stage. They both held a handful of one dollar bills in one and a Hennessy on the rocks in the other. They had shared an ecstasy pill and where both rolling into freak mode.

As they tipped the sexiest strippers, Toni noticed as Cody approached. He was one of the most lucrative dope boys in the city, and Toni could smell money a mile away. She nudged Coco with her elbow and nodded in his direction. Coco knew this meant it was time for them to put on their sexiest show.

From that moment on, they enticed the strippers with money while fondling body parts and seducing one another on stage. This instantly got Cody's attention as he walked over and showered Toni and Coco with hundreds of dollar bills. They tongue kissed each other while keeping direct eye contact with Cody.

They enticed him for the next hour and a half, and when he left, they left with him. The women followed Cody and his crew to his house in South St. Louis. When they arrived the partying commenced. Drinking, smoking, pill popping, they did it all. Toni even snorted a few lines of Cocaine before the night was over.

While Cody and five of his friends watched, Toni and Coco began kissing and touching on another.

"Suck her pussy!" One of the male voices yelled to Coco to influence her to go further. She lifted Toni's skirt to reveal no panties and a clean shaven vagina. Her mouth watered at the sight and the cheers from the men added peer pressure to the equation. She licked and sucked Toni into oblivion as the men watched with the lust of cavemen.

After the drugs and alcohol, Toni was barely coherent, so when she climaxed into Coco's mouth, she hadn't notice that some of the men had already revealed themselves and were masturbating. By that time, Toni's head was spinning and she needed some air. She headed outside for air as Coco proceeded to give head to one of the men with his penis already out.

Toni stumbled out to her car and fell asleep in the driver's seat. When she awoke, she couldn't remember where she was or how she got there. She drove until she recognized a street sign and went home. She never looked back on that day.

Toni wasn't aware of what happened to Coco that day, until now. Coco made sure that Toni experienced everything that happened to her that night. Coco explained every gruesome detail of what Cody and his friends did to her before they put her out in the streets, raped and beaten.

"I didn't know." Toni was barely able to say through what felt like broken ribs.

"And you didn't give a damn! You don't care about shit but yoself. That's why when I ran into your friend and found out I'm not the only person you done fucked over, it made this a lot easier." Coco told her with sinful delight.

Toni's eyes were starting to swell completely shut as an image appeared in the doorway.

"I figured since you like to fuck, I'd help you get some dick!" When Toni heard the voice she knew that Peaches had to be the friend Coco spoke of.

Toni wept to herself at the thought of all the people she had wronged and how it would affect the outcome of this situation. She remembered a prayer David taught her, The Lord's Prayer. As she cried, Toni asked God for forgiveness and said The Lord's Prayer aloud to herself. To Coco and Peaches her word sounded like gibberish and they left the room thinking she had slipped into delirium.

The six men had done their duty and they left the warehouse to the women to finish their business.

"What we gone do with her?" Coco asked Peaches. Since becoming involved, she seemed to act as the leader of the duo.

"We can leave that bitch here. Leave the pictures and the video tape here too. They'll never trace this back to us. She half dead anyway, plus this is the eastside, it'll take forever for anyone to find her." Peaches schooled Coco.

The two women took time to wipe down anything that they or the men had touched, except for Toni. As one last gesture of hate, the women took turns urinating in buckets, then poured it over Toni's head.

"Die in piss bitch!" Peaches said before spitting in Toni's face. Coco followed suit before following Peaches out of the building and leaving Toni there to die. But she couldn't hear them. All she heard was David's voice quoting scripture.

Titus 3:4+5 "But after that the kindness and love of God our savior toward man appeared, not by works of righteousness which we have done, but according to his mercy he saved us, by the washing of regeneration , and renewing of the Holy Ghost."

She felt her life slipping away, but still managed to whisper. "Father forgive me." Before she finally slipped out of consciousness.

Pre-Occupation

While Brandon and Ivey sat down to dinner with her dad and step-mother, Ivey seemed to be somewhere else. It bothered her that after a week, she still hadn't heard from Toni. She had already decided that after dinner she was heading directly to her apartment.

"So Mr. Danes, Ivey and I were hoping you would do us the honor of giving Ivey away at the wedding? That makes you an official part of the wedding party." Brandon said looking for Ivey to agree.

"Is that what Ivey wants?" Randy asked also trying to get some sign that she was on board with what Brandon was saying.

"Um Um!" Brandon cleared his throat and kicked Ivey underneath the table.

"Huh?" Ivey snapped back into the conversation." I'm sorry, what did you say?" She said to the table, not even sure who she was addressing.

"I was telling your dad that we wanted him to give you away at our wedding." Brandon repeated to her.

"Oh yes dad, it would only be appropriate that you do."
She said very nonchalantly while playing with her food
with her fork.

"Are you sure about that?" Randy said noticing her
preoccupation.

Ivey realized that her worry could have been mistaken for
rudeness. She stood and put her napkin on the table.

"I'm sorry everybody. Yes dad, I really do want you to
give me away at the wedding, I'm just not here right
now. I have to go." She met Brandon at her dad's, so
they rode in separate vehicles. Brandon ran after her to
figure out what could possibly be more important than
their wedding.

"Ivey!" He shouted as he ran after her. "Where are you
going?" He caught up to her at the front door.

"I need to find Toni!" She finally said out loud as she
turned to face him.

Brandon sighed as if to imply "Here we go again." But
Ivey stopped him in mid-expression.

"Look Brandon, I know you have an issue with my sister,
but she's my sister and I know something's wrong! I
didn't ask you to come because I know how you feel
about her, but I have to go. I haven't talked to her in
over a week, and she hasn't called me, period, that's not
like her." She was clearly riddled with concern.

"I'm going with you." Brandon said without a thought.

He didn't care how he felt about Toni, just looking at the concern in Ivey's eyes was enough for him. Brandon briefly explained the situation to Randy and they both jumped into Brandon's car headed to Toni's.

When they pulled in the parking garage, Ivey noticed Toni's car parked in a space close to the door. She felt instant relief at the thought that Toni was at home safe in her apartment. They made it to her door and after about two or three minutes of waiting, Ivey decided to use her spare key to let herself in.

Once inside the loft, she realized Toni wasn't there. The place looked abandoned. Besides the furniture and the sound of the electricity, there was no sign of life. Her first reaction was to call Romero. He was the only other person she knew might be able to help her find Toni.

His phone rang until the voicemail picked up. Ivey left him a short message to call her when he got a chance. She didn't want to put anyone into panic mode, but she was having a difficult time keeping herself calm. In fact, she had never felt so helpless.

She wanted to call the police, but what would she tell them? "I put my sister out of my house a week ago and now she won't call me?" "Yeah right, that'll spark urgency," Ivey said under her breath.

She took one last scan around the apartment to see if she missed anything. There was no sign of Toni's luggage so she prayed she was on another one of her phantom out of town trips.

"Let's go." Ivey told Brandon walking toward the door. She decided her next move would be to call the hospitals. Then if all else failed, she would continue to pray for her sister, wherever she was.

Beautiful Nightmare

She was out of breath, but continued to run as fast as she could toward the light that seemed to get further the closer she came to it. And she ran, the hair on the back of her neck stood up at the threat of someone on her heals. She heard breathing. It got closer. She tried to run faster, then she realized the breath she was running from was her own.

It wasn't until she stopped running that Toni realized she was alone. She looked around to try and get her bearings, but nothing looked familiar. She continued toward the light at the end of what seemed like the longest darkest tunnel in the world. When she got close to the light, Toni could hear voices.

"Hello?" Toni said toward the light that seemed to blind her the closer she came. "Somebody please help me!" She pleaded then suddenly began to get weak. She started to feel pain piercing through her body. When she looked down, blood began to soak through the clothes she was wearing. Toni was in full panic mode as she finally penetrated the light to reveal Coco and Peaches sitting around a table with the six men that raped her.

She moved in what seemed like slow motion as she turned around to run back into the darkness. Her heart seemed to beat out of her chest. But when she reentered the doorway, she stood alone in her loft apartment. She touched everything as she walked to make sure they were really real.

All she wanted to do was take a bath. Instinctively, Toni walked toward her bathroom to make an attempt to wash off all she had been through.

BOOM! BOOM! BOOM! It sounded like someone was trying to tear down the walls. Toni instantly began to cry uncontrollably. She crouched down into a ball on the floor. She knew this was the end.

"This must be hell." She cried thought snot and tears. She closed her eyes to await what was coming next.

"Toni! Toni!" She heard a familiar male voice, but was afraid to open her eyes. Then she smelled the stench of urine and must in the air, and realized once she tried to move, that she was still tied to the bed she had been so savagely violated on. She was in more pain than she remembered as she tried to open her massively swollen eyelids. She could see the image of what looked like and angel at first.

"Ro-mer-o? Are you real?' Toni had hallucinated so much during her capture, that she wasn't even sure what was real or fake.

But this time it was real. Since moving away from Toni, Romero had to be sure he could protect her, no matter what. He had GPS installed on Toni's I Phone that he and Jojo had access to, and made sure they knew where she was.

After watching the signal for three days without moving, Rome knew something was wrong. If he knew anything about Toni, he knew for a fact that she would not stay in one place that long.

Rome and Jojo frantically removed the ropes from her legs and wrists.

"Yes baby, I'm real." Rome said while gently kissing her forehead.

Romero wanted so badly to question Toni as she lay with her head in his lap while Jojo sped through the St. Louis streets trying to get to St. John's Mercy Hospital. She lay moaning as Rome tried to recognize Toni through blood, bruising, and swelling.

As tough as he was, it took everything in him not to shed a tear as he looked at his once drop dead gorgeous companion endure excruciating pain and cling to life. He felt so sorry for her that he hardly noticed the stench as he looked at her face.

Both her eyes were swollen shut and her jaw appeared to be broken. She could barely move her mouth but her face hurt so badly, she didn't want to.

Rome wanted so desperately to know who had done this to her. He didn't care why, he just needed to know who and he would handle everything else from there. But, in the meantime, he had to make sure Toni would live to give him the information he so desperately desired.

Toni was instantly admitted after triage into the intensive care unit of the hospital. Her physical damaged reached far beyond what could be seen. There was severe internal bleeding, broken ribs, dehydration, pneumonia, a broken jaw, missing teeth, Chlamydia, not to mention the emotional damage.

As soon as Toni was stable in her room, Rome contacted Ivey. He didn't want to alert her to the severity of Toni's condition over the phone, so he only provided basic information about the hospital and where to locate them.

Jojo however, sat quietly in the ICU waiting room. He couldn't believe someone had hurt Toni the way they did. And even more, he hoped Peaches was not involved. Romero was out for blood from anyone involved in what happened to Toni, and he was sure Peaches would not be exempt. He still hadn't received a return call from Peaches, but he hoped he talked to her, before Romero was able to talk to Toni.

The Calm

The journey to the hospital seemed to take forever. After talking to Romero, Ivey immediately had Brandon escort her to St. John's. Rome gave her very little information about Toni's condition so all she could do was pray for the best.

Ivey couldn't help but to think back to the gut feeling she had that Toni was in some kind of danger. And although she was relieved that Toni was getting help, she was actually nervous to find out why her sister had been missing in action.

Brandon let Ivey out at the door so he could find a parking space. The anticipation of seeing Toni gave her butterflies. Against her better judgment, she decided to head to the ICU department alone. She saw Jojo first as she entered the corridor. He stood to greet her with a hug when she noticed the look on his face, before he sat down and put his face back in his hands.

His clothes were covered in blood and Ivey's stomach dropped, she was not ready to face the fact that the blood belonged to Toni.

"Where's Romero?" Ivey asked Jo as Brandon walked up behind her and rested his hands on her shoulders.

"He in there with Toni. I think she can only have two visitors at a time, so only one of yall can go back." He said pointing to Brandon.

"I'll wait here baby, go ahead." Brandon said kissing her on the forehead before taking a seat in the waiting area.

Ivey walked down the corridor. The white walls seemed to go on forever. She finally reached the open doorway to the Intensive Care Unit. A nurse with a clipboard approached her.

"How can I help you?" The friendly nurse asked.

"I'm here to see my sister, Antoinette Danes." Ivey replied.

"Right this way." The nurse led her to the room closest to the nurse's station.

When she turned the corner, the first thing she saw was Romero sitting next to the bed holding Toni's hand. The closer she got to the bed, she realized why everyone acted as if they were grieving. Toni was hooked up to so many IVs and contraptions that Ivey feared she was on life support.

"Oh my God!" Ivey couldn't believe what she was seeing. She hoped the nurse had made a mistake, but she knew she had not.

Romero stood to embrace Ivey, but in her disbelief, she walked right past him and up to Toni's bed.

"Toni, can you hear me?" Ivey asked praying for a response.

"No, she can't Ivey. They put her in a drug induced coma because of her pain and loss of blood. She's had two blood transfusions already and they hope it'll be enough to get her blood count where it should be." Rome tried to repeat what the doctors had told him verbatim.

"What happened to her?" Ivey said with a knot in her throat.

"I'm not sure. According to the doctor, she's been raped and beaten, but I don't know who or why. But when I find out…." Rome got quiet for fear of incriminating himself. He paced the floor like the answers to his questions were engraved in the tiles.

"God can handle whoever did this way better than you can Romero." She told him trying to discontinue the violence.

"Fuck that! Whoever did this shit is gone pay, my way!" He tried to contain the volume in his voice.

Ivey knew this wasn't the time to attempt to reason with him, so she focused her attention back to Toni. She looked at the woman lying in the bed and tried to see any remnant of her sister.

Her face alone was so disfigured that if her name wasn't on her chart, Ivey would've thought she was in the wrong room. She gently rubbed Toni's forehead taking care not to hurt her. Ivey said a short prayer over her.

"Father God, please restore my sister, your daughter, remove all fear and doubt from her heart by the power of your Holy Spirit, and may you Lord, be glorified through her life, in the name of your son, Amen." Ivey wanted to cry but she knew she needed to be strong for Toni. Even Romero said a silent "Amen" when she finished her prayer.

She excused herself into the hallway to make some calls. First, to her dad, she knew that he and Toni's relationship was strained, but she was still his firstborn child. Ivey was even surprised at the devastation in his voice after she told him about Toni's condition.

She gave her father directions to the hospital and proceeded to call David. She knew that he had become somewhat close to Toni, plus she needed him to be a prayer warrior for them all. As far as they knew, he was also the last person to see Toni before she disappeared. So, Ivey was sure he would be happy to know they found her.

"Hello, Deacon James? This is Ivey. I hope I'm not interrupting anything?" Ivey said making sure he wasn't busy.

"Of course not sistah, what's on your mind?"

"We found her." Ivey said bluntly.

"I'm happy to hear that, I was beginning to really worry." He said with concern.

"Well I'm not sure how good it is. She's in ICU with a plethora of injuries, in a drug induced coma." Ivey began to feel the weight of the situation on her shoulders and in her chest. Everything seemed so surreal, and repeating what Romero told her made her feel sick to her stomach. She was about to break down, but she had to try to contain her emotions.

"Just pray for us Deacon please." Ivey was able to say while she held back tears. She was so caught up in her own emotions, she hadn't thought about how what she just said, may have affected David.

"Where is she? A coma? What happened to her?" He said almost in a panic. He was not prepared for what he just heard.

"Oh, I'm sorry Deacon. We're at St. John's Mercy. We don't really know what happened. No one's been able to talk to her yet." Ivey said feeling slightly sorry for him.

"I'm on my way. Are you holding up okay?" David said with concern for Ivey.

"I'm hanging in there. It's just so surreal, you know." She said wanting to awake from this nightmare.

"Yeah, I'm having a hard time processing all of this myself. But I'll be praying all the way there, see you shortly." He assured her.

After they ended their call, Ivey just stood, not really sure what to do next. She didn't want to think, thoughts kept taking her to a place where Toni doesn't make it. So she occupied her thoughts with actions. She entered Toni's room.

"I'm going to Toni's to get some personal items. She wouldn't want to be seen dead in this hospital gear. And I'm spending the night." Romero tried to protest but Ivey cut him off before he could get one word out.

"I'm family so I'm sure you won't force me to pull rank, Rome. But I promise, if they wake her up while you're gone, you'll be the first person I call." She said before leaving to go to Toni's apartment. She didn't want any resistance from Romero, so she left without giving him a chance to respond.

When she and Brandon returned, the visitors that had arrived to see Toni sat waiting for their turn to go in. By this time, David, her dad, and step mother had arrived. They sat anxiously for either Jojo or Rome to come out of the room. Brandon and Ivey greeted everyone with hugs and handshakes.

Ivey talked to the staff to make provisions for her to stay with her sister, then alerted Romero and Jojo that Toni had other visitors. As David and Randy passed Rome and Jo on the way to Toni's room, David remembered his first meeting with Jojo. The memory was as unpleasant as the feeling he got when they passed one another. He realized Jojo remembered him as well when he heard him whisper. "Square ass nigga." Out loud to himself.

When they entered the room, David's heart broke at the sight of Toni. Randy however, broke down and ran to Toni's side. He apologized for everything he ever thought he did wrong. Any guilt he ever felt surfaced right there.

David walked over to comfort Randy and to pray for Toni to be rejuvenated in her mind, body, and spirit. He had a strong feeling that not only would Toni survive, but she had some serious work to do.

Before leaving the room, David kissed Toni's cheek. She was the first woman he had kissed since his aunt died. Then he whispered in her ear, "He's not done with you yet."

Awakening

After being alone and out of contact with anyone for three days, Red decided to go back to New York. She didn't know where Romero and Jojo had gone and Peaches still wasn't answering her calls.

It seemed unlikely that everything was related, but the coincidence was too much. She tried to call Romero one last time before heading to the airport. There was still no answer. As she left another message, her cab approached the house. She was off to the airport and on her way back to New York,

She now regretted her decision not to tell Rome about the baby. "Maybe he would've stayed home." She thought.

Either way, she waited long enough for his return home and his return call. At this point, she didn't know if she should be worried or furious, but she knew she was returning to the comfort of her own home.

Her flight home was a blur of thoughts about what she should do next. A doctor's visit was the first thing on the list, but after that she was lost. She wanted to be making decisions with Romero, instead she felt like someone's thrown away baby's momma.

Red was glad to be home. She missed the hustle and bustle of New York City. She took in the sound and smell of the city as she walked up to her apartment building. Her phone vibrated in her purse as she walked through the lobby. With luggage in her hands, she let it go to voicemail and decided she'd return the call when she got into her apartment.

She barely got through the door before her phone began to ring again. This time she dropped her luggage and retrieved her phone from her purse. She was relieved to see that it was Peaches.

"Girl, where the hell have you been?" Red interrogated her without saying hello.

"Well, hi to you too." Peaches replied with an attitude.

"Really, you gone act like I haven't been calling you for a week? Well I guess it's safe to say you're okay?" Red said trying to contain her anger.

"Yeah, I'm okay, but I can't say the same for everybody." Peaches sang deviously.

"What are you talking about, Peach?" Red inquired.

"I'm talking about Toni's ratchet ass. That bitch should be rat food by now." Peaches said smiling ear to ear.

"Rat food, what the fuck did you do? You know what, never mind, I don't wanna know. Have you seen or talked to Jojo or Romero? Red asked.

"No, ain't you in Atlanta? Why would I have seen them?" Peaches was confused as ever and concerned about Romero's whereabouts in respect to Toni.

"I just got back to New York. Romero stormed out the house a few days ago saying he had some business to handle, and I haven't seen or heard from him since. I've been sitting in that big ass house alone!" Red said starting to get emotional.

Peaches sat quietly. She hoped Rome's business was far away from St. Louis.

"Are they in the Lou?" Peaches asked.

"I don't know where they are Peaches but I need to talk to him." Red voice sounded distraught.

"What's wrong?"

Red sighed before she answered. "I'm pregnant." Red looked down at the floor and tears started to fall.

Peaches on the other hand was ecstatic. She was more happy about the fact that Red's baby's daddy had money, than the fact that she was about to be an aunt.

"Jackpot Bitch! What the hell you soundin' so sad for? Shit, with Toni out the way, and you havin' that nigga's baby, bitch you finna be on a pedestal." Peaches said excited about the wrong thing. But the comment infuriated Red.

"You're a dizzy broad, you know that? I'm not planning a family around how much child support I can get from a nigga. I don't need Romero's money. I want Romero, period, to be my man and a father to our child. You can settle for that "I'm the number one bitch" shit, if you want to! And I don't want to hear shit else about Toni!" Red was furious at this point.

Peaches patiently waited for Red's rant to end before commenting. "You didn't seem so high and mighty when you were Mr. Grant's number one bitch. You gone find out one day that yo shit stinks just as bad as everyone else's" Peaches said smirking to herself.

"Fuck you!" Red yelled right before she hung up.

In her rage she called Romero's phone. She was determined to communicate with him one way or the other. When he didn't answer she left a message.

"Romero this is Red. I'm at home now and I don't really know how to feel about you leaving me alone for almost a week without checking on me. I'm not sure what's going on but I need to talk to you as soon as you find time for me." Red hung up the phone wondering if her calls made a difference.

She couldn't understand how the man she had grown to love, was acting like she didn't exist. Then she thought about what Peaches said about Toni. Red knew that Toni held a special place in Romero's heart. And if Rome's disappearance had anything to do with Toni, she shuttered at the thought of knowing that her sister was involved.

St. Louis

Toni could hear children playing in the distance. She looked around the field of wildflowers she stood in the midst of. She ran toward the sound of the children when she noticed two little girls playing in the distance. The closer she got, she realized as she approached the younger of the two, that it was Ivey.

She was dressed in an all white sundress looking more beautiful than she ever remembered seeing her. Then as the other little girl approached, she recognized the homely younger version of herself. She wore a tattered grey dress covered with dirt and holes.

"There's more to what you see you know?" Young Ivey said to her.

"What?" Toni looked down at the little girl with confusion.

"Toni!" She heard off further in the distance. She saw a woman standing on the porch of a house that resembled the one she grew up in.

"Toni, their waiting for you!" This time she recognized the woman. It was her mother.

"Mom?" Toni began to feel the desperation of loss and began to cry.

"Toni!" She heard her name again. Only this time it wasn't her mother. A flash of light took her back to the reality of the ICU. She struggled to open her eyes at the sound of her sister's voice. Then she felt a piercing pain in her side. She screamed out in pain as Ivey ran to the nurses' station.

"She's waking up!" She told the nurse.

The doctors decided to let her awake from the coma, and she had been struggling to awake for a couple of days. They were afraid that she had slipped into a permanent coma.

The staff rushed into action as they retrieved the necessary instruments needed to work on Toni. Ivey ran back to the room to check on her sister.

"Toni, the doctors are on their way!" She said frantically.

Toni lay there motionless. Her eyes were open, but there were no signs of life. The medical staff rushed past Ivey to work on Toni.

Ma'am can you please wait outside, we will come and get you as soon as she's stable." A nurse told Ivey as she escorted her out the door. Ivey watched in horror as the doctors and nurses worked to revive Toni. She fell to her knees outside the glass doors of Toni's room and cried from her soul.

Brandon had just returned from the cafeteria when he heard the commotion. He almost dropped the food before sitting it down, when he heard Ivey's desperate cries. He ran to her side and picked her up from the floor.

"Baby, what happened?" Brandon tried to find out what transpired during his absence.

"I don't know, she was waking up and I went to get somebody and when I came back she wasn't.....doing anything!" Ivey was crying and barely audible. She was talking so fast Brandon barely understood what she said.

"Calm down, Ivey. Take a deep breath." He grabbed her shoulders and tried to gain eye contact.

Ivey couldn't control her emotions or her breathing. She began to hyperventilate and then blacked out in Brandon's arms.

When Ivey awoke, Brandon was right by her side.

"Where am I? Where's Toni?" She immediately jumped up from the bed in the observatory room. She completely ignored the pounding in her head.

"She's still in ICU. They stabilized her." Brandon tried to get her to lay back down.

"Relax Ivey. The doctors said your blood pressure is high and the stress of everything can make you sick. I need you to rest for a minute. I talked to Romero, he knows she's awake and he's on his way." He assured her.

"But if she's awake, I need to see her." Ivey struggled to get up, but Brandon stopped her.

"I've watched you put yourself through hell in the past week, and I know your sister is important to you, but you're important to me. All I'm asking is that you lay down and rest for a little while, please." Brandon pleaded with her.

Reluctantly, she laid back down. "One hour!" She said insistently. She tried to relax in order to appease her fiancé. She didn't want to admit it, but she knew he was right.

David sat next to Toni's bed holding her hand as he prayed for her healing physically, mentally, and spiritually. He held his head down as he prayed in silence, when he felt a gentle touch to the side of his face. He was startled momentarily and quickly looked up to see Toni looking at him.

"Hey you." Toni said to David almost in a whisper.

Before speaking he stood up and kissed Toni's forehead. The kiss held the emotion of a kiss to the lips and she felt it.

"I'm praying for you Toni." Was all he said before Romero entered the room hoping to see Toni awake. David stood as Rome entered and they stood face to face.

They both had the best intentions for Toni, but they stood on opposite sides of revenge. David stood strong in his faith that revenge belongs to the Lord, but Rome on the other hand, felt he was that vengeance.

"I need to talk to her alone. If you don't mind, bruthah." Rome said sarcastically.

David turned to Toni. "I'll be right outside, I'm not going anywhere." He assured Toni.

As Rome approached her bedside, he could still see the significant damage that had been done to her face.

"Hey babe, can you hear me?" Rome asked as he gently held her hand. She nodded to indicate that she understood.

"First I wanna tell you I love you and I'm sorry I wasn't there for you." He felt a knot in his throat as his words escaped it.

"No, it's not your fault." She could barely be heard over the machines. Romero move closer as she continued to speak. "I've done things that have come back to haunt me. I hurt people Rome, even you." She admitted.

"Whatchu mean? You haven't done anything to me that deserve this." He pointed at her from head to toe.

Tears began to flow down her cheeks. "I'm so sorry. Please forgive me." She looked at Romero with the eye that wasn't still swollen shut. "I slept with Jojo." She confessed still crying.

Romero clenched his jaw so tight, he almost cracked a molar. He removed his hand from hers and took as step back.

"So, Jojo had something to do with this?" Romero was trying to understand.

"No, Peaches, and Coco." She told him.

He was so confused he was beginning to develop a headache. He rubbed his temples to try to release the tension.

"But you were raped, who did that? And what does Coco have to do with Peaches and Jojo?" He asked trying to put the pieces together.

Toni slowly recalled the events that she could remember. She even told him the story of Coco's rape. Even though her body and will had been broken, she continued with the self-inflicted torture of believing she deserved what happened to her.

Romero sat next to her and listened to the horrific details. He was upset with Toni, but his love for her would only allow him to give in to his feelings of pity. But his anger however, was kindled toward Jojo and Peaches, and whoever Coco was of course.

He only expected so much loyalty form Toni, but Jojo had to know this would not end well. As soon as Rome stepped in the hallway, he dispatched his contacts to get the word on the street. He intended to make everyone involved in what happened to Toni pay a price he was sure they couldn't afford.

Toni had waited patiently for Ivey to visit. After Romero left, she actually felt slight relief because of her confession. Her body however, was still riddled with pain. She refused to look in a mirror for fear of what she would see. If the pain she felt was any indication of her injuries, she knew she had to look like a monster.

She really wanted to see her sister but she wasn't sure where their relationship stood at the moment. Toni just knew she was sorry for everything she had done to Ivey and couldn't wait to tell her.

Her mind drifted back to the moments as she woke up from her coma. She remembered the two little girls and tried to discern what everything meant. "There's more to what you see?" Then she remembered the young version of herself looking like someone's orphaned child.

Toni realized at that moment that she has never recognized her true worth. She had abused herself, more than anyone else in her life and there was so much more to life than what she thought was important. But now she was able to see the value in her life and the value of the people she loved. She knew now that she had to love herself in order to take her life in the direction it should be headed.

She heard someone enter her room and she just knew it was another nurse coming to poke or prod at her some more.

"Toni?" Ivey said as she approached the bed slowly. "You up?" Ivey asked.

"Hey little sister." Toni could hardly get out. She had only been awake about an hour, and it was already starting to take a toll on her battered body.

"Oh my God!" She then rushed over to the bed. She wanted to grab her and hug her but knew she couldn't without hurting her further. "I thought I had lost you." Ivey began to break down again as silent tears ran down her face as she looked at her sister.

"Don't cry sister. I'm here and I'm sorry. I'm sorry for everything I've done to you. I've been so hateful and vindictive that I didn't realize I had my best friend here all along. I love you so much Ivey." Now Toni had tears flowing as well. Both women cried as they held hands and discovered a relationship anew.

The Storm

After Romero called Jojo and told him that Toni was awake and he was on his way to the hospital, Jojo went into all out panic mode. He had been trying to reach Peaches for almost two weeks.

He hadn't seen the children and was worried about them. But even more, he needed to find out what Peaches knew about Toni. He even went to her apartment and came up empty. So empty that not only did his key not work, but the neighbor told him Peaches had moved, with no forwarding information. Jo knew he had to find out where she was before Rome did. He knew her disappearance could not be a coincident. So he stayed as far away from the hospital and Romero as possible until he found some answers.

He decided to call Red. He figured she would know how to reach her sister.

"Wuz up Red? I was wondering if you know where Peaches is." Jo asked.

"Nothing's up. But it amazes me how I'm eight hundred miles away and everyone keeps asking me about people's whereabouts. Nobody's calling to check on me, just to question me about somebody else! I don't know where anyone is! And I'm a tell you like I told her, FUCK YOU!" Red screamed before hanging up on him.

"Damn!" Was all he could say as he looked at his phone like he could see damage from her hang up. What she said replayed in his head. "Everybody keeps asking me about people's whereabouts." It was apparent that she was talking about Peaches. But what puzzled him was, who was Peaches looking for and why. All he knew is that she wasn't responding to him.

Her parents' house was his next resort. He pulled in front of the run down two family flat that was in the heart of the westside of St. Louis. He noticed two children running in his direction. Just as he realized it was Raina and Ryan, he heard them screaming.

"Daddy!" He bent down to embrace them both and picked them up in his arms at the same time. He hugged them, and then put Ryan down. They did their special handshake that Jojo taught him and kissed Raina on the cheek.

"Where yo momma?" Jojo asked the children. They both shrugged their shoulders. "Okay, where's you Grandma?" He questioned some more. Both children pointed to the house.

"Okay, go play." He said while putting Raina down beside her brother. They both took off running down the street to play with their friends.

He was about to knock on the door when Peaches' mother Brenda, came walking up to the screen door blowing cigarette smoke into Jojo's face. She was fat, high yellow, and unattractive. Although, he heard that back in the day she was finer that Peaches on her best day, but not now.

"Whatchu want Jordan?" Brenda said calling him by his government name.

"Um, hello Mrs. Mason, I was just wondering if you knew where to find Peaches?" He said putting on his best Eddie Haskel impression.

Brenda looked around her body, inside her robe, and in her robe pockets.

"Nope, she ain't around here. Besides, do you really think I'm finna tell you anything if you gotta ask me?" She told him before taking another puff to blow out in his face. "You comin' to get these kids?" She asked.

"No ma'am, I'm just trying to get in touch with Peaches right now. Can you please tell her to call me?" Jo asked.

"Yeah nigga, whateva." She said dismissively as she turned around and walked back into the house.

"Fat ass bitch." Jo said under his breath as he walked away.

It was a matter of hours before Romero got the information about the individuals involved in Toni's assault. All six of the men were related to Coco. Four brothers and two cousins and all Romero could think was, "This gone be one big ass funeral." He also knew where to find Coco and Peaches. Apparently Peaches had moved to a house in Chesterfield, and she and Coco had been inseparable.

He couldn't imagine how Peaches obtained the money to move to that part of town. He knew Jojo gave her money, but not enough to maintain a house worth almost a million dollars. And as far as his contacts knew, she didn't live with anyone, which made it easier for him to carry out his plans.

Relieved he had gotten the information he desired, he decided to take a moment to listen to his voicemail messages. He had about four different voicemails from Red. They all however, expressed her non-appreciation for his lack of communication. He wasn't sure where she stood in all of this, so he decided to keep her at a distance for now.

There was already a plan in place for Coco's family members, before Rome took his trip to Chesterfield. He found out vital information about the family. The men that raped Toni were small time drug dealers that lived in the dope house they sold from. Rome lived by the

"Don't shit where you eat" concept, so he knew he was dealing with amateurs in the game. To be sure his plan went the way it should, Romero parked at the end of the block to watch as his instructions were carried out.

The dope fiend he paid to execute his plan had just turned the corner and was making his way to the door of Toni's assailants. The Brown boys, so everyone called them, had a dope house that sat right in the middle of the block. Rome made sure to find someone they were familiar with so they didn't think it was strange when he knocked on their door.

Knock. Knock. Knock.

"Fuck is it?" A male voice yelled from the other side of the door.

"Black!" The fiend yelled back.

Troy, the oldest of the men, opened the door to let him in.

"Whatchu want?" Troy asked as he mean mugged Black.

"A twenty, but lemme use yo toilet man, I gotta piss." Black said bouncing up and down to indicate as such.

"You get yo dope, when you come out, I don't want you smoking that shit in my house." Troy told him as he pointed in the direction of the bathroom. No one even noticed that Black wore a jacket even though it was eighty five degrees outside.

Black walked into the bathroom, which didn't smell much different from the rest of the beyond filthy residence. He took care in removing the C4 from his jacket. He strategically placed it underneath the bathroom sink. Romero had paid him five thousand dollars for the job and he felt it was worth risking his life to get the money.

Black washed his hands and flushed the toilet. His heart was pounding out of his chest. He wanted to be out of this house and far enough away when Romero detonated the C4. He finished his transaction and quickly left the house.

Romero watched as Black walked in his direction, giving him the sign that the coast was clear and that the Brown boys were alone. Rome pulled out of his space and drove to the next block. He hit the red button on his remote and watched through his rearview mirror as the house went up in flames. He smiled with satisfaction as he made his way to his next destination, Chesterfield.

Jojo had to resort to connects of his own that had no connection to Romero, which proved to be a difficult task. But luckily, he was able to find information on Peaches' new place of residence.

He also found out that Peaches had purchased a new white Lexus Coupe. With the details he was given, he almost thought he was getting information on the wrong person. The source of the information however, let him know this was the same old Peaches.

Since Jo was no longer a part of the equation, Peaches took the liberty of inviting any and every one she slept with to her house. So finding her address was much easier than it should have been. "Dumb ass girl." Jojo said out loud while punching her address into his GPS.

They Meet

Saturday nights were the busiest at the Pink Slip Strip Club in East St. Louis. Peaches needed to clear her head after finding out about Toni and Jojo, so she went out to the club alone. She tried to arrive early enough to get a seat, but when she got to the club the line was down the street.

Peaches was glad that she decided to wear Chucks with her True Religion jeans and BeBe tank top instead of the Sergio Rossi T-strapped sandals she almost wore.

"Hey!" Peaches saw a girl at the front of the line trying to get someone's attention when she saw the girl's familiar face.

"Hey you, come here!" The girl said again pointing directly at Peaches.

Before losing her place in line she wanted to be sure the girl was talking to her.

"Me?" Peaches mouthed as she pointed to herself.

The girl nodded. The closer Peaches got, she recognized her from the last night she and Toni went out. She sighed at the thought that she had to endure drama because of someone she no longer considered a friend. When she got close enough to talk, she addressed Coco.

"Look, I don't know what you and Toni got goin' on, but I don't fuck with her no more, walking, running, or skipping." Peaches told Coco with an attitude and one hand on her hip.

Coco immediately cracked a smile that spelled conspiracy.

"You ain't gotta stand in that line girl, come in with us." Coco said pointing to the crowd in front of her.

"It don't surprise me that yall fell out, she ain't shit." Coco said.

"You can say that shit again." Peaches replied.

"Fuck all that, we bout to kick it. I'm ready to turn up." Coco put her arms up and did a quick dance to the faint sound of music she could hear coming from inside the club. "We in V.I.P., you should roll wit us." Coco offered.

"That's cool." Peaches agreed.

They spent the rest of the night smoking, drinking, and tipping strippers. It wasn't until the next morning at breakfast that Coco revealed her plans for Toni. Although hesitant at first, the thought of Toni and Jojo made her livid all over again and she was on board as if she had planned Toni's torture herself.

Since plotting against Toni together, Peaches and Coco had become new best friends. And the fact that they pleasured one another on a regular basis made their bond much stronger than just friends. Although they didn't live together, Coco spent more time with Peaches than her own children.

They lay in bed, both wearing boy shorts and tank tops, watching television when breaking news of an explosion in St. Louis City caught their attention.

"That's my cousin's house!" Coco said suddenly sitting up in bed.

"That is my cousin's house!" This time she pointed at the television then covered her mouth in horror.

"Late breaking news of an explosion in the 5700 block of Blackstone in West St. Louis City. Five adult males were found burned to death in the home." The sound of the male news caster's voice blasted through the speakers.

"Oh my God, I need to call my auntie!" Coco began frantically stirring around the room to find her cell phone. Peaches sat helplessly and in horror as she watched the EMTs rolled five body bags out of the house.

"The explosion is currently under investigation." Was the last thing they hear the news caster say before the bedroom door came crashing in almost off the hinges. Both women were so startled they almost jumped out of their skin.

"Romero, Wha what are you doing here?" Peaches asked reluctantly.

"I should be asking you the same thing." Romero said looking around obviously talking about the house.

"I mean, how did you know I was here?" Peaches was clearly shaken and afraid, and Rome could see it.

"That's the least of what you should be worried about me knowing. You Coco?" He asked looking in Coco's direction. She just nodded, she was too afraid to speak. She just held onto a pillow for dear life; she knew exactly who he was.

"So I guess that means you haven't talked to Jojo either?" He smirked. "Who you running from Peach?" He moved closer to the side of the bed where she sat.

"I ain't running from nobody." Peaches said nervously. She tried to read Romero by his eyes and facial expression, but it was impossible.

"You talked to Toni?" He decided to test her reaction.

"Toni?' She repeated.

"Yeah, you remember Toni?" He said sarcastically.

The question sparked an unexpected flame in Peaches.

"So you leave my sister alone so you can find that scandalous hoe? Just so you know, yo lil angel been fucking Jojo!" She raised her voice involuntarily.

"You could write a book with what I know. Like how Toni wound up in an abandoned building on the east side, raped and damn near dead." Rome now examined both the women's expressions.

They were both horrified when the words parted his lips. But the true horror was revealed when Romero retrieved a 9mm from the back of his pants. Coco instinctively tried to run, but was met with a blow to the face with the butt of his pistol. She dropped to the floor like a rag doll.

"Pick this bitch up!" He ordered Peaches with a wave of his gun.

Peaches helped Coco off the floor and back to the bed. By that time, they were both sobbing uncontrollably. But he had no sympathy. All he could think about were those same tears and sobbing coming from Toni while they watched as six men violently assaulted her. The thought alone further infuriated Romero.

"Both you bitches shut the fuck up!" Romero screamed this time cocking his gun. The sobs turned into pleading.

"Please Romero, I got kids." Peaches said holding her hands up like they could block a bullet. Coco still held the pillow tight to her body while she cried into it.

"Aw yeah, where the fuck are they then? You so busy spending time with this jump off." POW!

In an instant Coco's body slumped over the pillow she was holding and blood began to soak through it. He shot her in the head, but he had never taken his eyes off of Peaches. They burned a whole right through her.

Snot and tears covered Peaches' red, swollen face. She curled up in a ball at the head of the bed next to Coco's body; splatters of blood were on her clothes.

"Please Romero, I've got money. I'll pay you!" She pleaded with desperation.

"It ain't enough money to erase what you did to her from my memory." He said through clenched teeth, now pointing the gun directly at Peaches.

POW! A bullet entered her left knee.

"AAAAAHHHHH!" Peaches screamed in excruciating agony.

POW! The second bullet ripped through her left shoulder, throwing her body against the head board. Another blood curdling scream erupted from Peaches' throat. Romero walked up to her and put the barrel of the gun to her temple.

"I just need to know one thing; did Red have anything to do with this?" He asked Peaches

She was bleeding profusely but still managed to look up at him.

"No." She responded as blood came from her mouth as she spoke.

Before ending her life, Romero had to be sure that Red didn't deserve the same fate. He operated on pure vengeance and emotion at that point and hadn't even processed the fact that he was about to murder his woman's flesh and blood, nor did he care. He repositioned his gun and put his finger on the trigger.

"What a waste." He said looking down at Peaches.

Just before he could apply enough pressure to send a bullet through her brain, Jojo appeared in the doorway out of breath and toting a 9 mm of his own. He looked around the room at the massacre in progress.

"Man, what the fuck you doing dog?" Now Jojo's gun was pointed at Romero.

"So first you smash my bitch, then you pull a gun on me! Nigga you must be crazy!" Romero's gun was still pointed at Peaches.

"Man, don't do this please!" Jo tried to plead with him as well.

"Too late, it's already done."

POW!

Romero pulled the trigger, shooting Peaches in the head. Her body slumped over Coco's.

Jojo's heart began to pound. Everything seemed to move in slow motion. As if it were a natural reflex, Jo pulled the trigger hitting Romero in the stomach. He didn't even realize he was hit when adrenaline and anger took over as he returned fire hitting Jojo between the eyes.

Jo dropped his gun and fell to his knees before finally falling face down on the floor. Romero looked down to notice blood staining his T-shirt. He tried to stop the bleeding with his hand as he stumbled out of the house and into his car.

He heard sirens in the distance as he felt his life slipping away. He picked up his phone and called Red. The phone seemed to ring forever when she finally answered.

"So you finally found time for me, huh?" Red said with an attitude, very confused about her feelings.

"I'm sorry Red. I'm sorry for everything." Romero said coughing up blood into his hand.

"I'm sorry too." Red replied.

"For what?" He asked barely conscious.

"Cause I didn't tell you about your baby." She struggled to say.

"Baby? My baby?" Romero said in a whisper as the phone fell from his hand.

One month later

Once the police contacted Red's family about the Chesterfield ordeal and Red was placed in charge of Peaches' estate, an attorney contacted her about Peaches' last will and testament.

When she arrived in St. Louis she was still confused about so much. Like how Peaches had an attorney and a will. Not to mention, the gruesome details of Romero's revenge. She was upset with him for his attempted murder of her sister, but she knew that Peaches wouldn't go unpunished for the things she had done.

She went to the lawyer's office directly from the airport. Although Peaches had survived, she was declared incompetent to take care of herself or the children. She also had severe brain damage from the gunshot to the head and loss of oxygen to her brain.

Once Red arrived at the attorney's office, she was bombarded with the overwhelming news that not only had she been awarded guardianship over Peaches and her two children, she also found out that her sister had over two million dollars in her bank account.

"The house in Chesterfield is yours as well. It's paid for." The attorney told her while handing her keys to the house and the Lexus.

"Where did she get all this money?" Red asked the attorney.

"Ms. Mason, I am not at liberty to discuss matters that transpired before your sister became unable to handle her own affairs. However, I am prepared to continue on as your attorney." He told Red handing her a business card. Red took the card and put it in her wallet. She extended her hand to the well-dressed middle aged white man.

"Thank you Mr. Mueller. I will let you know if I'm in further need of your services." Red said as they shook hands.

After leaving the office, she decided it best that she go to the house before picking up her niece and nephew. She wanted to be sure that everything was in order and that there were no signs of the tragedy that occurred there.

When she arrived, she pulled into the circular driveway behind the white Lexus Coupe. As she exited her rental, she admired the beautiful specimen of an automobile and made a note to herself that her first trip would be to return the rented Camry.

When she walked up to the steps, she took notice of the beautiful traditional brick home. When she walked into the foyer she was amazed. The décor was elegant and the design of the house was beautiful. But Red was still baffled as to how Peaches gained this kind of wealth.

She took a stroll around the house to inspect the cleaning company's work, which she hired. They specialized in unusual clean ups. Red specified that she didn't want a trace of tragedy left in the house. She had to admit they did an excellent job. If she hadn't known where the shooting took place, she would have never had a clue.

Red went from room to room, either admiring or redecorating in her head. It was really all she could do to avoid thinking about the responsibilities she had been left with. The baby she'd be forced to raise alone, her niece and nephew, and not to mention caring for a mentally and physically disabled adult. The thought alone was overwhelming to her, so she tried to focus on other things.

Her transition back to St. Louis would be among the first things she would need to focus on. She wanted the children's transition to go as smoothly as possible. They were strong little children and she admired their resilience.

Red whirled down the spiral staircase and was instantly reminded of Romero. As much as she missed him, she couldn't help but be furious with him for risking everything for Toni. Then she rubbed the small bump starting to form in her belly.

"We gone be alright." She said to her unborn child. She continued to explore her new home, observing every nook and cranny, when she came to a huge locked wooden door. She retrieved the skeleton key from her pocket and proceeded inside.

She was astonished by the beautiful cherry wood furniture in the office. The bookcase, the desk, and the cherry wood trimmed leather sofa, complimented every inch of the room. As she looked around, she noticed an envelope marked confidential in bold red letters.

She picked up the envelope to reveal the contents inside. Red carefully went through each document with a fine tooth comb. The papers were years' worth of bank statements with large deposits made each month. Next to each deposit Red saw "MEALTICKET" written in red ink.

"Meal ticket, Peaches what you up to?" Red said to herself as she continued looking through the paperwork. The marked bank statements seemed to date back about four years and the deposits got larger about three years ago.

She turned page after page until she noticed a document with a familiar name and logo, Rebman & Associates. She squinted to make sure her eyes didn't deceive her. She held a check stub for $1.5 million.

Her heart began to pound as she retrieved the final document sticking out of the envelope. A look of horror was etched across her face. Red could never remember feeling as sick as she did at this moment. She dropped the paper on the desk and then threw up in the trash can next to it.

Morning sickness could not compare to the sickness of the betrayal printed on the document.

Paternity probability for Raina Mason 99.9%
Paternity probability for Ryan Mason 99.9%

Jonathan Grant is not excluded as the father of Raina and Ryan Mason.

The Rest of Me

It had been about four weeks since her last visit from Romero. Toni text him and called every day, but still there was no answer or reply to her calls and texts. She had been trying to put the pieces of her life back together and truthfully, Rome didn't fit into the new life she was trying to establish. But that fact made her worry about him no less.

Ivey was at the hospital every day; even her graduation couldn't keep her from visiting Toni. Brandon's support during that time was phenomenal, he wasn't just there for Ivey, and he gave Toni nurturing support as well. It seemed the family in general was forming a long overdue bond. Toni, Randy, and Regina had made amends and had begun to start developing an actual parent child relationship. Regina knew she could never take the place of Toni's mother, but at least it was a start.

David also visited Toni everyday, but the relationship they had was something more spiritual than anything either of them had ever encountered. David stayed true to his word about having a physical relationship but there was nothing he could do about his emotions. In the beginning, he would sit for hours and watch her sleep while he prayed for her physical and spiritual well-being. He missed their conversations and was ecstatic the first day she was able to stay awake longer than a few minutes.

"Did they admit you too?" Toni asked sarcastically. He seemed to be there every time she opened her eyes and she was grateful.

"Yep, their charging me to be roommates with you, funny lady. How are you feeling?" He asked as he stood up from the chair and walking to her bedside.

David instinctively grabbed Toni's hand. He had done that every day for the past month, so it wasn't as out of place for him as it was for Toni. She hesitated before speaking as she watched David's intimate gesture toward her.

"I don't feel much of anything right now. How do I look is the question?" She moved her tongue around in her mouth. "Am I missing teeth?" Toni asked in a slight panic. She was too drugged to act the way she truly felt.

"That's not important right now; nobody cares how you look except you. To be honest with you Toni, your vulnerability makes you more beautiful than I've ever seen you." David gently rubbed the side of her face with his hand as he spoke.

He looked into her eyes so deeply; she felt he could see her soul. Her normal reaction to a man she was attracted to would start between her thighs, but she felt like she was on a nonstop roller coaster ride when it came to David. She was speechless, all she could do was return his stare, she didn't know what to say.

"I want to share something with you Toni." He released her hand long enough to retrieve and open his bible, then he resumed his affection.

"Ephesians five one through twenty says, Be ye therefore followers of God, as dear children; And walk in love, as Christ also hath loved us, and hath given himself for us an offering and a sacrifice to God for a sweet-smelling savor. But fornication, and all uncleanness, or covetousness, let it not be once named among you, as becometh saints; neither filthiness, nor foolish talking, nor jesting, which are not convenient: but rather giving of thanks. For this ye know, that no whoremonger, nor unclean person, nor covetous man, who is an idolater, hath any inheritance in the kingdom of Christ and of God. Let no man deceive you with vain words: for because of these things cometh the wrath of God upon the children of disobedience. Be not ye therefore partakers with them. For ye were sometimes darkness, but now are ye light in the Lord: walk as children of light: (For the fruit of the Spirit is in all goodness and righteousness and truth;) Proving what is acceptable unto the Lord. And have no fellowship with the unfruitful works of darkness, but rather reprove them. For it is a shame even to speak of those things which are done of them in secret. But all things that are reproved are made manifest by the light: for whatsoever doth make manifest is light. Wherefore he saith, Awake thou that sleepest, and arise from the dead, and Christ shall give thee light. See then that ye walk circumspectly, not as fools, but as wise, redeeming the time, because the days are evil. Wherefore be ye not unwise, but understanding what the will of the Lord is. And be not drunk with wine, wherein is excess; but be filled with the Spirit; Speaking to yourselves in psalms and hymns and spiritual songs, singing and making melody in your heart to the Lord; Giving thanks always for all things unto God and the Father in the name of our Lord Jesus Christ;"

As David read the verses, Toni closed her eyes and listened with her heart. She was aware that some serious changes had to be made in her life. As she absorbed the Word, her mind drifted back to the people, places, and things that caused her life to travel in a downward spiral. She realized the primary culprit was her and she had to change or she was afraid it would mean her life. Then her mind drifted to Romero. Toni couldn't understand why he had disappeared the way he did. When David finished reading he focused his attention back on Toni.

"So, did you understand?" He asked her sounding like a true Deacon.

"Yes, it means I'm going to hell." Toni joked.

She was being facetious but after she heard what God had to say, she wasn't sure if she would make the cut. David chucked at Toni's comment.

"No it doesn't. It means that we serve a merciful God that will forgive us for everything if we choose to walk in his light. I know the concept of God's mercy seem too

good to be true, but it's not. In fact, it's as true as our existence. And he loves us more than we love ourselves." David explained. "This is spiritual food and I want you to eat it." David said when he got up and walked over to a folder on the nightstand. He had blown up the bible verses and printed them. "I want you to be able to read this every time you open your eyes." He said as he retrieved tape from the room's supplies and commenced to taping the papers on her hospital room walls.

"Thank you David, thank you for caring." Toni said as an emotional lump formed in her throat and a single tear ran down the left side of her face.

"You don't have to thank me. This time I'm not doing you a favor, I needed to be here, for me. I needed to see with my eyes that you're okay." He told her.

They stared at each other for what seemed like an eternity, but it was only a silent few seconds. Toni didn't know how to feel. She wasn't accustomed to being treated like more than a sex object. Hearing and seeing genuine love and concern gave her an unfamiliar but warm feeling inside.

"Where's Ivey?" She asked changing the subject conveniently.

"She was here earlier while you were resting; she said she'll be back." David told her returning to his chair but this time moving it to Toni's bedside. "I'll be here until she comes back." He assured her.

They talked and laughed until Ivey arrived half an hour later. Toni was ecstatic to see her.

"Hey Chickadee!" Toni squealed calling Ivey by the nickname she gave her as a child.

"Hey sis, how are you feeling?" Ivey walked over and kissed Toni on the cheek.

"I'm better, I guess. Are those for me?" Toni said excitedly referring to the balloons and flowers Brandon entered the room with.

"Yes ma'am, it's time to replace these." Ivey worked diligently to remove old flowers and replace them with new ones. She also disposed of the deflating balloons and replaced them as well. "A cheerful atmosphere promotes healing and high spirits." Ivey told her.

"I need to talk to Ivey in private if you guys don't mind." Toni said to David and Brandon.

"Of course, I'll be in the waiting area." David said.

"Me too babe." Brandon told Ivey.

As they exited the room Ivey sat in the chair next to Toni's bed.

"What's up sis?" Ivey said giving Toni her undivided attention.

"Have you talked to Romero?" Toni asked.

Ivey looked down at the floor and fiddled with her fingers. Toni searched for her eyes and tried to determine the reason for her actions.

"Ivey!" This time Toni's voice was elevated.

"No, I haven't. But I wanted you to get better before I told you this; Romero didn't handle what happened to you very well." Ivey said while she tried to gage Toni for a reaction.

But all she saw was a blank stare, waiting for an answer to her question. Toni lay on her back but the look on her face made Ivey's hair stand up on the back of her neck. Ivey took a deep breath.

"He shot Peaches, Coco, and Jojo and according to police, his blood was found on the scene as well, but there was no body recovered. They even found his rental car, and it was covered with blood on the inside but there was no sign of Romero." Ivey hesitated with every word while she watched her tortured sister's face change emotions as she spoke.

"He killed them?" Toni asked with horror etched in her face and her voice.

"Coco and Jojo are dead, but Peaches is in really bad shape. She'll be mentally and physically disabled for the rest of her life. Rome was also suspected in the deaths of Coco's cousins that raped you too. Their house exploded, in broad day light."

When Ivey finished talking, Toni cried in silence. Tears flowed freely down her cheeks but she didn't make a sound. She felt the guilt of the effects of her actions. All of these people were dead because of her, and she felt undeserving of her second chance at life.

Happily Ever Afters
(six months later)

Ivey and Brandon's wedding was pushed back three months due to Toni's injuries. Toni and Ivey had forged a new relationship and were closer than they had ever been. For the first time in her life, Toni started to love and respect Ivey for who she was. She also appreciated having genuine love in her life, not someone she wasn't sure she could trust or that was around because they expected something from her other than mutual love and respect.

Toni had taken so much for granted and she was grateful to God that she would finally be able to really live her life for the first time. She hadn't realized it, but until now, she had never really been happy.

Her scars had healed; she felt and looked like a new woman. What nature didn't heal, Toni got plastic surgery to fix. Her looks however, were no longer what made her who she was, God did. But she had to admit that Deacon David James helped a little.

She was experiencing many firsts in her life; being an active member in church, being an active member of her family, and being an active member of a relationship without sex. And although it was one of the hardest transitions she had to make, she was actually up to the challenge and was proud of herself for her discipline.

There were no more drugs and alcohol in her life, although she had the occasional slip and would sneak a joint from time to time. "Gotta crawl before you walk." Is what she'd say to justify her actions? But she would have never imagined that her life would be where it is now.

She and Brandon were actually getting along like sister and brother, and she had even developed a productive relationship with her father and step mother. Her lengthy recovery made it impossible to attend Ivey's graduation, but she was there in spirit.

In her relationship with David, he taught her about forgiveness. And that God forgives her by the measure that she forgives others. So the past six months of her life had been dedicated to the development of new relationships and the restoration of old ones.

But there was still one relationship that she had yet to mend. And that would be the one between her and Red. She felt they shared somewhat of a bond because of the tragedy that affected them both. But Toni still felt responsible for the chain reaction that was caused by her actions. She even wished she could let Peaches know that she had forgiven her for what happened.

Toni stood in the dressing room of the church admiring how beautiful Ivey looked in her wedding dress. Her hair was pulled up into an elegant bun and she was in the middle of getting her make up applied. It was a fall wedding, so Ivey picked a gorgeous lace and satin Vera Wang gown with lace ¾ length sleeves. The gown fit her tall slender frame perfectly. Toni got a lump in her throat as she tried not to cry at the sight of her not so little sister getting ready for the first day of the rest of her life.

Toni walked away to get her composure so she wouldn't mess up her own make up. She checked in on the bridesmaids, then took a peek into the audience to see how many guests had arrived. She saw that the church was almost full when she noticed an eight month pregnant Red sitting on the bride's side of the church.

As she made her way to Red, she noticed how pregnancy gave her a glow that actually made her more attractive than she'd ever seen her.

"Hello Red." Toni said extending her hand. Red looked her up and down with slight hesitation and disbelief. "I'm glad you could make it." Toni continued as if she didn't notice Red's reaction.

"Hi." Red finally said reciprocating the gesture.

Toni looked at Red's stomach in admiration. She had long ago accepted the relationship between Red and Romero in an effort to have a relationship with God.

"I saw you from the back. I really just wanted to tell you how sorry I am about what happened. I feel like I single handedly turned you and the kids' lives upside down." Toni said hanging her head in shame.

"Toni, as much as I try, I can't blame you for anything. The bottom line is, you didn't deserve what they did to you, my sister included. I admit, it hasn't been easy, but I believe things happen for a reason. My relationship with Raina and Ryan is closer than I believe it ever would have been. Plus, they have a stable home now." Red told her.

"How's Peaches doing?" Toni asked with hesitation.

"Well, she's not doing much of anything. She can't walk or talk and she pretty much has a care giver a majority of the time. I'm limited in what I can do, of course thanks to this lil boy." Red said pointing to and then rubbing her big belly.

"Congrats." Toni said to Red then moved closer before asking her next question. "Has there been any word on him?" She asked but never said his name. Red knew who she was referring to.

"Not other than the car they found about five miles from the house, covered in blood. There still hasn't been a body recovered though." Red was visibly saddened at the thought that he could be out there and not contacting her.

"I'm sorry, I didn't mean to…."

"It's okay." Red cut her off in mid-sentence. "We'll be okay." Red said as if she was talking to her belly.

"You and the kids should visit church some time" Toni said trying to lighten the mood.

"Well, that's not really my thing but I'll definitely think about it." Red said.

"Keep in mind that even if you don't wanna come you can bring the kids anytime. They'll be in good hands." Toni assured her. "I gotta go back to finish getting ready. Will you be at the reception?" Toni asked.

"I planned to make an appearance." Red smirked. She wasn't sure how she felt about this conversation with Toni. But as off putting as she tried to be, the new Toni that stood before her gave off a positivity that was contagious.

"I hope to see you there." Toni said extending her arms for a hug. As Red returned the hug, Toni whispered to her. "I just want you to know that we are sisters in Christ and I'm here for you if you need anything, remember that." She gave Red a slight squeeze before she headed back to continue getting dressed.

Red was in awe of the person she had just come in contact with. She couldn't believe that the girl she could barely stand to be around just made a positive impression on her. Her usual mistrust for women, never even came to the surface.

After putting on her maid of honor gown, Toni went to check on Ivey. When Toni walked into the room Ivey was fully dressed and ready to get married. Her makeup was flawless and her white beaded Vera Wang sling backs made her look like a runway model. Toni smiled with the real pride of a big sister.

"This is it. You're about to be Mrs. Cameron. You ready?" She asked Ivey.

Ivey looked Toni deep in the eyes with the seriousness of a heart attack. "I've never been so ready for anything in my life. I'm finna run down this isle."

"Well, I have something for you. I didn't want everyone making a big deal out of it, but here's your wedding gift." Toni handed Ivey a white envelope.

She opened the envelope to reveal a seven day trip for two to Le Meridien Bora Bora overwater bungalows in Tahiti.

"Oh my God, thank you so much!" Ivey screamed. Toni found out through their much needed conversation that Tahiti was her dream vacation.

"It's the least I could do. Despite everything I've done, you've been there for me and nursed me back to health. I still don't feel like its thanks enough but it's a start. You deserve it lil sis." Toni gently hugged her little sister and lightly kissed her on the cheek, taking care not to mess up her dress and make up. "Well let's get this show on the road." The sisters walked to their designated location to start the ceremony.

As Toni walked down the aisle with Brandon's older brother Chris, she was amazed at how many people came to honor Brandon and Ivey's union. People loved Ivey and she could finally see the person that everyone else knew. She was observing life and was no longer so wrapped up in herself. Now she could actually see the forest without the trees.

The reception at The Moonrise Hotel was even more beautiful than the wedding. Everyone mingled and danced after eating the delectable buffet style meal. Even Red attended as discussed. The best man stood and clinked his fork to his glass.

"May I please have everyone's attention? I would like to make a toast to the bride and groom. I'll make this short and sweet. I knew Ivey would be a part of my family the first day this dude came home talking about her. I had never in life heard him talk about a woman the way he did about her. The stupid look on his face alone was enough to let me know this was it. So I say to you lil sis, welcome to the family Mrs. Cameron!" Chris said toasting with Brandon and Ivey.

Then he continued. "And we have one more announcement this evening." David approached Chris and took the microphone.

"Good evening everyone. I would first like to say congratulations to the bride and groom." He turned to Ivey and Brandon and provoked an applause. Then he turned his attention to Toni.

"I feel like I've taken the longest journey of my life to find you. I always say, I'll be with a woman when God send her to me. And you Ms. Danes were sent like a bullet, and what doesn't kill you makes you stronger, right?" The guest erupted with laughter. "But seriously, I can't imagine my life without you. You're more amazing than you even know and I love you more than I even knew I would." David reached into his jacket pocket as he got down on one knee. Gasps could be heard from every corner of the banquet hall. "Antoinette Danes, will you please marry me?"

Toni was crying uncontrollably by the time he got to the question. All she could do was nod her head yes over and over until he placed the two carat diamond ring safely on her finger. After wiping her tears and admiring her ring, she was finally able to speak. "I would be honored to be your wife, Mr. James."

The Honeymoon

The three flights it took to get to Tahiti took a total of about twelve hours. Ivey and Brandon were exhausted and couldn't do anything but sleep once they finally arrived. They were so tired, they hadn't even notice how beautiful their island destination was.

Six hours later, Ivey awoke to the most beautiful dawn she had ever seen. She stepped out onto the private deck to admire the atmosphere. The sun barely peeked over the mountain when she noticed how clear the tropical waters were. She couldn't wait to swim with the colorful fish that she could clearly see in the clear blue ocean.

On the way back inside the bungalow Ivey noticed that the floors in the bedroom and living room had glass see through panels. It was like a dream of paradise come true. Every aspect of it was more beautiful and exotic than she could have ever imagined. She contained her excitement and went to the bathroom to shower.

Warm water ran down the front of her body while she held her head back and allowed the shower to hit her chest. Ivey closed her eyes and tried to relax. As excited as she was to make love to Brandon, she was twice that nervous. Just as her nerves began to calm she felt hands gently rubbing her shoulders, then lips gently kissing the back of her neck. She let out a soft moan of pleasure.

Brandon grabbed her waist and rotated her body to face him. He kissed her passionately then proceeded to wash her from head to toe. He took care not to miss a crevice as he teased and caressed all her sensitive areas. Ivey moaned even louder as the moisture between her thighs multiplied by the second. He rinsed her body soap free and then dropped to his knees. He carefully leaned her against the wall as he lifted her left leg over his right shoulder. Brandon gently placed his lips around her throbbing wetness, while stroking it with a stiff tongue. Ivey couldn't control her body or her breathing.

"Oh my God!" She cried out as she held the back of Brandon's head while pumping his face.

Ivey's porn star moans had him so turned on, he almost released prematurely. He had to slow things down. So he picked her up and carried her to the bedroom. He laid her on the king sized bed and admired every inch of naked body for the first time.

"You are so beautiful." He spoke without realizing he had said anything out loud.

"Then show me." Ivey said seductively, jolting him from his trance.

He kissed and caressed her from head to toe. He wanted to make this night beautiful for Ivey. He was gentle and loving with every touch. Just as he wanted, she was dripping wet when he finally entered her. The initial pain was nothing compared to the pleasure that followed.

They made love well into the next day, and night. Ivey was happy, happy to be Mrs. Cameron and happy that saving herself was more than worth the wait.

Meanwhile, back in St. Louis

Toni sent her third text message to Ivey to make sure they make it safely, as her and David finished their meal at Toni's apartment. She had prepared her famous chicken lasagna that he fell in love with the first time she cooked for him.

"She won't respond." Toni said frustrated that she hadn't received a reply.

"Baby, now you know good and well why she's not responding. She doesn't even know where that phone is." David laughed at his own comment. But it took Toni a moment to snap out of protector mode.

"Yeah, I guess you're right. I know what I would be doing if I was her." She put her phone down deciding to stop the barrage of messages.

Now she focused her attention to her fiancé. She put her elbows on the table and sat her chin in her hands as she stared lovingly into his eyes.

"Now, tell me again why you love me?" Toni smiled at him while she waited for the response she loved so much. He put his fork on the plate and grabbed her hands as he looked deeply into her eyes.

"I love you because I'm Adam and you're Eve, plus my heart breaks when you leave. Then you show me a life with a colorful view, I could go on forever about loving you." David recited the words he said to her the first time he told her how he felt.

"I love it every time you say it. But I have to be honest with you about something; I've never been in love before now so all of this is new for me. I just ask for your patience." She said now rubbing his hands.

"Toni, all I ask is that you're honest with me, even if it's a painful truth. I've never felt this way about anyone either, so we're in this together." He said to her without breaking eye contact. She stood to clear the table and leaned across the table to give him a peck on the lips.

"I hear you and I promise." She said to him before heading to the kitchen.

David made his way to the living room to get comfortable and find a movie on Netflix. He was anxious about making Toni his wife. They planned a small wedding a month from now. In his opinion, waiting only prolonged the inevitable. Plus, he needed to be intimate with the woman he loved. But until then, they would remain abstinent.

Toni heard her phone go off. She rushed to the dining room table excited to see what Ivey sent back. But when she looked at her messages there was a phone number she didn't recognize. The text read,

"BECAUSE OF U, MY LIFE WILL NEVER BE WHAT IT WAS. ENJOY WHAT U HAVE NOW.....I'LL BE BACK!"

Toni stared at the message in horror and confusion.

"Was that Ivey?" David yelled from the living room.

"Um no. It was a wrong number." Toni stuttered as she lied.

She knew she promised to tell the truth no matter what, but she was afraid that she would drive away the only man she ever loved with her past.

"You okay, baby?" He asked recognizing the discomfort in her voice.

"Yes baby, everything's fine." She told David, but she knew nothing could be further from the truth.

Made in the USA
San Bernardino, CA
19 September 2018